Other Books by Harriet Steel

Becoming Lola

Salvation

City of Dreams

Following the Dream

The Inspector de Silva Mysteries

Trouble in Nuala

Dark Clouds over Nuala

Offstage in Nuala

Fatal Finds in Nuala

Christmas in Nuala

Passage from Nuala

Rough Time in Nuala

Taken in Nuala

High Wire in Nuala

Short Stories

Dancing and other stories

AN INSPECTOR DE SILVA MYSTERY

COLD CASE
in NUALA

HARRIET STEEL

Author's Note and Acknowledgements

Welcome to the tenth book in my Inspector de Silva mystery series. Like the earlier ones, this is a self-contained story but, wearing my reader's hat, I usually find that my enjoyment of a series is deepened by reading the books in order and getting to know major characters well. With that in mind, I have included thumbnail sketches of those featuring here who took a major part in previous stories. I have also reprinted this introduction, with apologies to those who have already read it.

Several years ago, I had the great good fortune to visit the island of Sri Lanka, the former Ceylon. I fell in love with the country straight away, awed by its tremendous natural beauty and the charm and friendliness of its people. I had been planning to write a detective series for some time and when I came home, I decided to set it in Ceylon in the 1930s, a time when British Colonial rule created interesting contrasts, and sometimes conflicts, with traditional culture. Thus Inspector Shanti de Silva and his friends were born.

I owe many thanks to everyone who helped with this book. My editor, John Hudspith, was, as usual, invaluable, Julia Gibbs did a marvellous job of proofreading the manuscript, and Jane Dixon Smith designed another excellent cover and layout for me. Praise from the many readers who tell me that they have enjoyed previous books in this series and want to know what Inspector de Silva and his friends get up to next encourages me to keep going. Above all, heartfelt thanks go to my husband, Roger for his unfailing encouragement and support, to say nothing of his patience when Inspector de Silva's world distracts me from this one.

Apart from well-known historical figures, all characters in the book are fictitious. Nuala is also fictitious although loosely based on the hill town of Nuwara Eliya. Any mistakes are my own.

Characters who appear regularly in the Inspector de Silva Mysteries

Inspector Shanti de Silva. He began his police career in Ceylon's capital city, Colombo, but in middle age he married and accepted a promotion to inspector in charge of the small force in the hill town of Nuala. Likes: a quiet life with his beloved wife, his car, good food, his garden. Dislikes: interference in his work by his British masters, formal occasions.

Sergeant Prasanna. Nearly thirty and married with a daughter. He's doing well in his job and starting to take more responsibility. Likes: cricket and is exceptionally good at it.

Constable Nadar. A few years younger than Prasanna. Diffident at first, he's gaining in confidence. Married with two boys. Likes: his food, making toys for his sons. Dislikes: sleepless nights.

Jane de Silva. She came to Ceylon as a governess to a wealthy colonial family and met and married de Silva a few years later. A no-nonsense lady with a dry sense of humour. Likes: detective novels, cinema, and dancing. Dislikes: snobbishness.

Archie Clutterbuck. Assistant government agent in Nuala and as such responsible for administration and keeping law and order in the area. Likes: his Labrador, Darcy; fishing, hunting big game. Dislikes: being argued with, the heat.

Florence Clutterbuck. Archie's wife, a stout, forthright lady. Likes: being queen bee, organising other people. Dislikes: people who don't defer to her at all times.

William Petrie. Government agent for the Central Province and therefore Archie Clutterbuck's boss. A charming exterior hides a steely character. Likes: getting things done. Dislikes: inefficiency.

Doctor David Hebden. Doctor for the Nuala area. Under his professional shell, he's rather shy. Likes: cricket. Dislikes: formality.

Emerald Hebden (née Watson). She arrived in Nuala with a touring British theatre company, decided to stay and subsequently married David Hebden. She's a popular addition to local society and a good friend to Jane. Her full story is told in *Offstage in Nuala*.

Charlie Frobisher. A junior member of staff in the Colonial Service. A personable young man who is tipped to do well. Likes: sport and climbing mountains.

CHAPTER 1

A thrill of anticipation ran through Inspector Shanti de Silva's veins as he and his wife Jane mingled with the crowd. The air smelled of petrol and vibrated with the revving of powerful engines being tested before the race. It was the day of Nuala's famous car rally, the Hill Country Challenge, and an area of the bazaar had been cleared of its usual stalls to turn it into the starting point. Celebrated as one of the most exciting events that the Hill Country had to offer, the rally took place once every four years and was customarily held in January when dry weather could be relied upon. Entrants came not only from the island. They also arrived from India and even further afield, attracted by the rally's prestige and the hope of winning the coveted trophy.

This would be the third time de Silva had attended, the first being shortly after he arrived in Nuala to take up his post as head of the Nuala police. Familiarity would, however, never dull the excitement he felt at the sight of so many magnificent cars – Bentley, Maserati, Riley, Lagonda, Talbot, Alpha Romeo, and Bugatti – and the famous names ran through his head as he admired immaculate paintwork and gleaming chrome sparkling in the afternoon sunshine. It had always pleased him that one of the first Ceylonese on the island to own a car was named Silva. He felt, in a small way, that it linked him to the history of the automobile in his country.

Of course, there had been huge advances since then. In the early years, there were barely two dozen cars on Ceylon's roads; now it was not so remarkable to own a car, although it was still the preserve of the better off. He was lucky that his job enabled him to afford his beloved Morris, but despite the fact that she would always have a special place in his heart, she couldn't compare with the cars assembled today. He had to admit that they were thoroughbreds.

'Gracious, how crowded it is,' remarked Jane. 'And what a noise the cars make.'

'But a glorious one. Like a pride of lions calling to each other. And it will be even louder once they're off.'

'Oh dear,' said a familiar voice behind them. 'I hope it won't become too much louder. I have one of my headaches coming on.'

They turned to see Florence Clutterbuck. For once, she was not carrying her little household mop of a dog, Angel. No doubt he would enjoy the occasion even less than his mistress claimed to be doing. De Silva's boss, Archie Clutterbuck, was also bereft of his usual shadow, his black Labrador, Darcy, but in contrast he seemed to be in his element. He looked smart in cream trousers and a navy blazer that had the badge of the Royal Automobile Association of Ceylon embroidered in red and gold on the breast pocket.

'Good morning to you, de Silva! And Mrs de Silva! A pleasure to see you, ma'am. Marvellous turn out, eh? My money's on the Bentley to win.' Archie gestured to a huge black beast of a car that dwarfed its rivals. He glanced at his wife. 'Not that I'm really a betting man, of course, but today's a special occasion.'

'Indeed it is,' said Florence in a sudden change of tone that, to de Silva's amused surprise, bordered on indulgent. 'We've just been talking with Johnny Perera, the Bentley's driver. Such a charming man. The son of Dudley Perera, you know.'

De Silva nodded. He had certainly heard of Dudley Perera. Who had not? He was reputed to be one of the island's wealthiest Ceylonese businessmen. So, this was his son. From the tales that sometimes crept into the newspapers, his nickname, the "playboy prince", was well deserved. His handsome features were animated as he chatted and laughed with the gaggle of admirers surrounding him, several of them extremely attractive young ladies. A well-manicured moustache set the seal on his dashing air. De Silva guessed he must be in his mid-thirties.

'Young Frobisher's here somewhere,' said Archie. 'He's back on leave for a few days.' He chuckled. 'Brought a very charming companion with him.'

'She's a WAAF based at China Bay,' said Florence. 'That's where they met.'

Jane smiled. 'How nice. I hope we run into them.'

They chatted for a while and admired the cars before parting company. 'Well,' said de Silva with a grin as they walked on through the crowds, 'perhaps your wish is coming true.'

'What wish would that be?'

'Charlie Frobisher. Haven't you been wanting him to find a suitable wife?'

She raised an eyebrow. 'It's really none of my business.' Her voice softened. 'But I'll admit, I'd be delighted to see him happily settled. He's such an engaging young man.'

By now the engines had fallen silent. Drivers and their co-drivers were donning leather helmets and goggles as their teams pushed the cars into their starting positions, angled side by side into the road, then they walked towards the starting line. Stewards with bull horns boomed instructions to the crowds. Moving like a sluggish river, they slowly crammed in behind the safety barriers that had been set up on either side of the start.

'Of course, things may not be so well organised all along

the route,' remarked de Silva as they squeezed themselves into a gap.

'Let's hope people have the sense to keep well back. I'm always afraid there will be some horrible accident.'

De Silva couldn't deny that rallying was dangerous. He suspected that the danger was a large part of the attraction for the rally drivers. That and the challenge of finding out what speeds they could attain when the roads were free of bullock carts, rickshaws, and errant pedestrians. These days, the most powerful cars were built to attain speeds of over one hundred miles an hour.

'Look!' he said excitedly. The starting steward held aloft the green flag, and there was a moment when the crowd seemed to hold its breath before the flag swooped down and, to cheers and shouts of encouragement, the drivers and their co-drivers raced from the starting line towards their vehicles.

Engines coughed into life and the air pulsated as the drivers opened up to full throttle and they were off! The smell of petrol intensified; de Silva's ears rang, and his heartbeat quickened.

The first part of the course required the drivers to negotiate a route through the intricate maze of narrow streets that made up the older, more traditional area of Nuala. It was very different in character to the parts the British had built. Those were in the colonial style with wide streets, pavements, and well-marked junctions.

However, once the cars emerged onto the town's perimeter road, also built by the British about forty years previously, they would be able to increase their speed. With the required number of laps of the perimeter completed, they would head up the hill to the racecourse. Finally, there would be a dash down the hill back towards Nuala and the finishing line. With the victorious car in the lead, the ones who had made it would then progress down the wide main street, finishing up in the square in front of Nuala's best hotel, the Crown, for speeches and the presentation of the trophy.

As the cars disappeared from sight into the labyrinthine streets, the crowd of spectators fanned out across town to watch from different places on the perimeter road. There were several well-known vantage points where the drivers had to use all their skill to stay in the race. Jane and de Silva installed themselves alongside the tricky bend close to the point where the road up to the Residence branched off. They didn't have long to wait before they heard a growl that soon turned into a roar.

'I might have to close my eyes,' said Jane anxiously.

'But then you'll miss the excitement.'

The jostling pack of cars streamed into sight, the Bugatti in the lead, flashing like a silver arrow. To de Silva's surprise, for he agreed with Archie Clutterbuck's assessment, the Bentley was only in fourth place, but then he decided that the playboy prince must be holding her back until later on. After all, there were many more laps and the last leg up to the racecourse and back to go. De Silva recalled him taking part in the rally before, so he'd probably worked out his strategy. He hadn't won on either of the occasions that de Silva had attended, but he had come close, and this time he had the advantage of the best car in the field.

The Bugatti negotiated the bend smoothly, followed by the Riley, the Alpha Romeo, and the Bentley. But when it came to the turn of the next car, the Lagonda, the driver took the bend too fast. A gasp rose from the crowd as the car went into a skid. For a moment, de Silva feared the driver would not be able to keep control. He held his breath, but then by some miracle the Lagonda righted itself and raced on.

The next few laps passed without incident, but on the fifth lap the Riley also skidded and overturned not far from where they were standing. Jane's hand went to her mouth. 'Oh, I hope the driver's not hurt. And what if another car comes along and runs into him?'

'Just watch. These people know what they're doing.'

The words were no sooner out of his mouth than, as if out of thin air, a group of men in overalls dashed onto the track. The driver and his co-driver were already halfway out of the car, and they hauled them the rest of the way. More men appeared with buckets at the ready. De Silva wasn't sure whether they contained water or sand, but fortunately, they were not needed. After some frantic pushing and pulling, the car was righted and wheeled to the side of the road. The operation was performed in the nick of time; a few seconds later, the next car roared past. Swiftly, men de Silva assumed to be mechanics checked the Riley over. As they did so, the driver and co-driver were already swinging themselves back into their seats.

'I think I'd like a cup of tea after all that excitement,' said Jane.

'I'm not sure where we'll find one out here.' De Silva glanced around him. 'But there's a stall over there that looks to be selling cool drinks.'

'Then that will have to do.'

They chose their drinks and de Silva paid the stallholder a few annas. Jane wasn't hungry, but he was tempted by another stall that displayed a variety of snacks. He chose some crispy vegetable rotis, fragrant with curry leaf and coconut, and the stallholder handed them over in a paper cornet.

'The Hebdens decided not to come this time,' remarked Jane as she sipped her mango juice. 'It's not long until the baby's due. All this standing about in the heat wouldn't have been good for Emerald. I shall have to hurry up and finish that shawl I'm making for the baby.'

De Silva had often seen her working on the beautifully

soft, cobweb-fine shawl. 'It does seem to be taking you longer than most of your projects,' he remarked.

'It's because the wool is so thin.'

They finished their drinks and de Silva ate the last of his rotis then left the empty paper cornet on the stall's counter. He looked at his watch. 'When you're ready, we might watch from somewhere else for a while. We'd better get up to the finishing line soon though if we're to have a chance of seeing it properly. There's bound to be a big crowd.'

Jane brushed a curl of carrot from the side of de Silva's mouth. 'I'm happy to go there now if you like. We might even find somewhere to sit down for a bit while we're waiting.'

De Silva tucked her arm through his. 'Very well.' He had long ago accepted that speed and the smell of petrol didn't carry quite the same thrill for Jane as it did for him.

It turned out that no benches were available, but not far from where the road down from the racecourse flattened out they found a place at a safety barrier with a decent view of the finishing line.

Jane took a pretty fan painted with flowers out of her handbag and began to fan herself. 'I wonder who'll win,' she remarked. 'If Archie really has put money on it, let's hope it's the Bentley. He'll be in trouble with Florence if he loses.'

'I don't think you need to worry. It's the most powerful car, and I expect young Perera has the race all worked out.'

People were gathering in ever increasing numbers in readiness for the end of the race. Stewards shepherded them behind the safety barriers as they arrived; already there was very little room left. A buzz of anticipation rose from the crowd. De Silva leant over the barrier, eager for the first glimpse of the frontrunners, the metal rail hot under his palms. A distant whine, like the sound of an angle grinder cutting metal, swelled to a roar then the first car came into sight. It was the Bentley.

'What did I say?' he shouted triumphantly over the din.

With the wind streaming past him, the playboy prince was almost unrecognisable behind his huge goggles. As he swung the Bentley into the finishing straight, he was already fifty yards ahead of the next competitor. De Silva and Jane watched the other cars fly past in a blur of silver, red, green, and blue. The sand-coloured dust kicked up by their wheels blew into the crowd. Jane's nose wrinkled at the grit and the smell of exhaust fumes. She definitely preferred the scent of Shanti's roses. Yet the excitement was infectious. She cheered on with the rest as the Bentley took the chequered flag.

By the time the next four cars finished, the Bentley's speed had dropped to a slow crawl. The playboy prince tugged off his leather cap and removed his goggles. His dark hair was plastered to his head and his face was coated with dust. Smiling, he accepted congratulations from the hordes of well-wishers now running alongside him. They draped garlands of marigolds around his neck and piled more flowers into the car until it looked like a garden on wheels.

All the other finishers were marshalled into a line. With the Bentley leading, they drove slowly towards the square. As he and Jane were swept along in the following crowd, de Silva noticed that Charlie Frobisher was not far ahead of them. They managed to catch up with him as the main street widened and the press of people thinned a little. He beamed.

'Good afternoon! This is a pleasant surprise. May I introduce my friend, Ruth Bailey?'

De Silva studied the young lady while the introductions were made. She was slim and pretty with dark, curly hair and an infectious smile. As the four of them continued along the street, she chatted to Jane while de Silva and Frobisher talked about the cars. Eventually they arrived at the square in front of the Crown Hotel. Red, white, and blue bunting had been strung across its façade and Union Jacks fluttered from the flagpoles. More bunting hung in scalloped garlands across the front of a dais on which a table had been set up. The Clutterbucks waited there with the senior officials of the rally's organising committee and their wives. De Silva saw that Archie had donned the elaborate chain of office that denoted he was the committee's president. On the table the coveted trophy, the Caldicott Cup, awaited the victorious driver. It was named after the wealthy tea planter and motor enthusiast who had founded the rally. There were also medals for those who had taken the second and third places.

The three drivers stood in a line while Archie made a short speech, but despite his booming tones de Silva found it difficult to make out what he was saying above the excited hubbub of the crowd.

'Can you understand a word?' he asked Jane.

She shook her head.

'I expect it's unlikely to be a great loss,' he whispered mischievously. 'Archie's not celebrated for his oratory.'

'So that's your boss,' said Ruth, looking both at Frobisher and de Silva. 'He looks very affable. Is he really?'

'Would you say so, de Silva?' asked Frobisher with a grin.

'Some of the time.'

Ruth laughed.

The speech over, Perera stepped up to receive the Caldicott Cup, shaking hands with everyone in the line until he came to Florence who stood ready to make the presentation. He certainly was a confident fellow, thought de Silva as Perera bowed to her with a flourish then turned briefly to the crowd and flashed a radiant smile revealing perfect teeth. Probably it would never occur to him that a lady, even one who could be as forbidding as Florence, would be impervious to his charms. In any case, this time he was right. Resplendent in a lilac dress with a cartwheel-sized, chiffon-swathed hat to match, Florence waited for him to turn back to face her and, when he did, favoured him with a warm smile of her own. Though too far away to be certain, he wondered wasn't that a blush appearing on Florence's cheek? De Silva thought it might well be.

'She must have gone home to change since we saw her earlier,' remarked Jane who stood at his elbow. 'Perhaps she wanted a little rest too,' she added, somewhat feelingly.

Perera turned again to the crowd and raised the trophy above his head. It gleamed in the sunshine and the crowd responded with cheers and applause.

'All over for another four years,' said de Silva smiling at Jane. 'You can rest to your heart's content now, my love.' He turned to Ruth Bailey. 'I hope you enjoyed the day, ma'am.'

'Very much so. It's been fascinating seeing the cars.'

'At the moment Ruth's working on administrative duties at the base. But she's applied to train for one of the crews that maintain and repair the aircraft.'

'That's marvellous,' said Jane. 'I'm sure you'll be very good at it.'

Ruth laughed. 'I haven't been accepted yet, but if I am, I'll do my best to be. In England, my family have farmed for generations. As a child, I was always interested in finding out how the farm machinery worked.'

The crowd was dispersing and already the reddening sun was half hidden behind the Crown Hotel's sprawling mock-Tudor façade. 'I promised Ruth a cocktail in the bar,' said Charlie Frobisher. 'We'd be delighted if you'd join us.'

For a moment, de Silva hesitated. He had never been into the Crown as a guest, only on official business. There was no reason why he shouldn't accept, but he dreaded any kind of awkwardness. Not all the British were like Charlie and Ruth.

'If you're sure we won't be intruding, we'd love to,' said Jane. 'Wouldn't we, Shanti?'

He overcame his scruples. 'Yes, it would be a great pleasure. Thank you.'

* * *

The bar at the Crown Hotel was crowded, but they found a table and were soon comfortably installed. Relieved to see that he wasn't the only local amongst the clientele, de Silva began to relax and enjoy himself.

In contrast to the entrance hall that, with its coloured glass ceiling, had a rather Art Nouveau air, in the bar the designers of the hotel had chosen the Tudor style of the building's exterior. The room combined baronial grandeur with comfort. Its ceiling was coffered in dark wood, and a dark-green paper patterned with tendrils and leaves covered the walls. Opposite the bar itself, there was a massive stone fireplace. It was decorated with brightly coloured and gilded heraldic shields, and the tawny gleam of copper fire accessories warmed its inglenooks. The grate was piled high with logs, more for effect, de Silva assumed, than from any real intention of lighting them. The air smelled of resin, mellow tobacco, whisky and well-aged brandy, with an underlying whiff of dog.

A waiter appeared bringing cocktail menus. As he looked down the list of exotic creations, de Silva saw that they had exotic prices to match, but Charlie Frobisher insisted it was his treat, and it seemed churlish to argue. All the same, de Silva ended up ordering a whisky and soda, but Jane was more adventurous and asked for a Mary Pickford. 'I've heard it was invented for her by a bartender at a hotel in Havana when she was on holiday there with her husband, Douglas Fairbanks, and their friend Charlie Chaplin.'

'Hmm; rum, pineapple juice, and grenadine,' said de Silva, raising an eyebrow. 'It sounds a little stronger than your usual sherry.'

'It's just what I need after standing all afternoon,' Jane countered, albeit with a smile.

Ruth decided to have the same, but Charlie, who preferred whisky to rum, chose an Old Fashioned.

As they chatted, de Silva discovered that Ruth Bailey had come out to Ceylon about a year previously. Before joining up, she'd lived with an uncle and aunt in Colombo and worked as a secretary at Government House.

'My uncle is retired now, but he came out from England forty years ago.'

'I'm looking forward to meeting him,' said Charlie. 'He spent all of his career in the Justice Secretariat, which is an area I'm interested in.'

Ruth smiled at him.

'And how did you like Colombo?' asked Jane. She took a sip of her cocktail. Served in a delicate glass, it was a pretty shade of pink, garnished with a maraschino cherry.

'It was interesting. Unlike anywhere I'd ever lived before. The Hill Country is much more peaceful though, and so beautiful. Charlie had already told me a lot about Nuala, and it's lovely to see it for myself.'

'Yes, Shanti and I prefer it up here. But when I first came to Ceylon, I worked in Colombo. Shanti was in the police force there.'

'Was that where you met?'

'Yes, it was thanks to my own carelessness. I was walking down the street one day, and I didn't notice a man following me until it was too late. He snatched my handbag and when I reported the theft to the police, Shanti was assigned to the case.'

'There had been a spate of thefts in that part of town,' said de Silva. 'Eventually we caught the gang, but sadly most of what they took, including Jane's handbag, was never recovered.'

'But Shanti was very conscientious about keeping me informed of his progress,' said Jane with a smile.

De Silva chuckled. 'I was trying hard to convince you of my abilities.'

'You certainly did that, dear.' Jane raised her glass to him and took a sip of her cocktail.

'Do you have lots of plans for your leave?' she asked Ruth.

'Charlie's already shown me some of the countryside and we go to Colombo soon. My uncle and aunt have asked us to visit them for a few days, but after that it will be time to return to the base.'

'What a shame. I hope it won't be too long before you come back again.'

'I hope so too.'

There was a commotion over by the entrance doors. De Silva looked up. It was Johnny Perera surrounded by an entourage of friends. With him also, and straining excitedly at its leash, was a large German Shepherd dog. Its cavernous red jaw opened wide displaying sharp white teeth as it let out a volley of barks.

De Silva recognised the man in formal evening wear who swiftly approached the group as being the hotel manager. He visibly flinched when the German Shepherd lunged in his direction, to be brought up short barely a foot away by the leash. A conversation ensued that resulted in the party being ushered through a door at the far end of the bar.

'It leads to one of the private rooms,' said Charlie Frobisher. 'No doubt the manager would prefer Perera's party to be safely contained there.'

They might be contained, thought de Silva, but whether they would be safe was another matter. Still, he doubted many people would begrudge Perera a celebration. He had driven magnificently.

* * *

'What a charming young lady Ruth is,' said Jane as they drove home later on. It was a balmy evening. Moonlight cast its beam on the road ahead, making it seem like a snaking river; the black velvet sky was full of stars. 'I hope we see her again.'

'I wouldn't be surprised.' De Silva raised a hand from the steering wheel to stifle a yawn. It had been a long day, although a very enjoyable one. 'She and Charlie seem to get on very well and to have a lot in common.'

'Yes. Both sporty and practical.'

Jane fell silent as they left the main part of town and reached the residential area where Sunnybank was situated.

'You're very quiet all of a sudden,' said de Silva.

'I was thinking about the war. It seems so far away in Europe. I'm ashamed to say I sometimes forget there's anything going on. Meeting Charlie and Ruth brings it all back and makes me fearful about what will happen.'

He reached out and squeezed her hand. 'I don't think there's any need to be afraid of the war touching us here.'

'I suppose you're right.' Jane sighed. 'I hope you are. I hate to think of lovely young people like Charlie and Ruth coming to harm.'

The Morris turned into Sunnybank's drive and when he'd stopped the car, de Silva got out and went to open Jane's door. She looked up at him. 'I'm sorry. I didn't mean to spoil the day.'

He kissed her cheek as he helped her out. 'You haven't. And I understand how you feel. I don't like the thought either. Now, shall we go in? I hope Billy and Bella haven't been getting up to mischief in our absence.'

He did understand, he thought, as they went inside, but the situation affected him differently. Even though as part of the British Empire, Ceylon was officially at war with Nazi Germany, her people had not seen action. Attitudes to the rule of the British had changed considerably since the

Great War. If the people of Ceylon were called upon once again to fight for the mother country, who knew how they would respond? In any case, he didn't intend to worry about events whose outcome seemed too far off to predict.

'Here they are,' said Jane. 'Sleeping like angels.'

Billy and Bella woke and stretched then came over to be stroked. De Silva reached down and picked Bella up. 'Have you missed me?' he asked.

Jane smiled. 'And you were the one who doubted we should have cats.'

CHAPTER 2

'Do you plan to go to church today?' de Silva asked as they sat down to breakfast the next morning. 'I'll drive you there and pick you up afterwards if you like.'

'It's very kind of you, dear, but I think I'll stay at home this morning. I'm a little tired after yesterday. I might try to make some progress on the shawl for Emerald's baby.' She looked up as one of the servants, a new addition to the staff at Sunnybank, brought the tea. 'Thank you, Leela. A poached egg on toast for me, please. The sahib will have his usual hopper and two eggs.'

'Yes, memsahib. It will be ready very soon.'

The eggs had no sooner been brought than the telephone rang in the hall. Leela reappeared in the doorway.

'It's a call for you from the Residence, sahib.'

De Silva's heart sank. He put down his napkin and pushed back his chair. A telephone call from his boss on a Sunday morning sounded ominous. The prospect of a restful day amongst his vegetables and flowers faded faster than morning dew under the tropical sun.

'I'd better take it.'

'Shall I take the eggs back to the kitchen to keep warm, sahib?'

'There's no need.'

In the hall, he picked up the receiver. 'Good morning, sir. Is there a problem?'

'You might say that. There's been a spot of bother up at the Moncrieff plantation. At the moment I'm not sure how serious it is, but we have to assume there needs to be further investigation.'

De Silva racked his brains, but the name Moncrieff meant nothing to him.

'Perera and some of his friends went up there last night after they'd had dinner at the Crown,' Archie continued. 'There was some business about him spending time there when he was a lad and wanting to see the place again. Why the thought popped into his head all of a sudden, I've no idea. Anyway, he took that damned great dog of his with them. It's only a young 'un, but totally out of control if you ask my opinion.' Archie paused for breath.

'Does anyone live at the plantation now, sir?' asked de Silva.

'Only Marina Moncrieff, and a few staff of course. She's the wife of Donald Moncrieff.'

'And he is?'

Archie gave a harumph. 'I'll explain all that in due course. The thing is, while Perera and his pals were having a look around the place, the dog slipped its leash. There was a hue and cry to find the beast. They heard it barking, that was how they tracked it, and at first they thought it had got itself stuck somewhere, but when they got to it, it wasn't in difficulties. It had been doing a bit of digging. Dogs are always finding some damn thing to dig up, y'know. Darcy has a fondness for it. The older and smellier the find, the better.'

De Silva waited for Archie to get to the point. He hoped he wasn't going to be treated to details of the archaeological interests of every dog his boss had ever known.

'De Silva?'

'Still here, sir.'

'Well, to cut a long story short, the dog, Caesar I believe

it's called, found some old bones. At first, Perera and his pals thought they were the remains of a family pet. But one of his group's a medic. It seems old man Perera insists on his son travelling with one when he's racing. Don't let on to David Hebden, but if his son has an accident and needs treatment, old man Perera won't have local doctors dealing with it. Anyway, this doctor fellow had his doubts about the bones. They found a few of the servants and got them to do a bit more digging around. It seems the bones may be human.'

De Silva groaned inwardly. As he'd feared, it was the end of his quiet Sunday.

'I'm going up to the plantation shortly,' Archie went on. 'I'll pick you up on my way. I can fill you in a bit more as we drive.'

'Very well. You said only Marina Moncrieff lives at the plantation now. Does she know what's happened?'

'I'm not sure. Apparently, she didn't come out to see what was going on, but Perera and his friends didn't arrive until late, and it was even later when they made their unpleasant discovery. Maybe the servants didn't want to disturb her. We'll have to find out more about that.'

'I'm not familiar with the plantation. Whereabouts is it?'

'Off the Kandy road. About ten miles from here.'

De Silva was puzzled. He must have driven that road a hundred times, but he'd never noticed it.

Back in the dining room, Jane looked at him sympathetically. 'Bad news?'

'It looks that way. It seems that Johnny Perera and some of his chums stumbled on a suspicious situation last night.' He explained about the dog and the finding of the bones.

'And the plantation belongs to a family called Moncrieff,' mused Jane. 'I know I've heard the name before. I think Florence may have mentioned a lady called Isobel Moncrieff, but she didn't speak of her warmly. If I remember rightly, she gave the impression that she didn't like her.'

'The lady Archie mentioned was called Marina. He said she was the wife of a man called Donald Moncrieff.'

'But presumably, Isobel is some relation.'

'Well, Archie will be here soon. He's offered to drive me up there, so I expect I'll find out more.'

He broke off a piece of his hopper and dipped it into the slightly congealed yolk of one of his eggs. The pancake had cooled, but it was still crisp.

'Would you like some fruit after that?' asked Jane. He shook his head. 'I don't think there'll be time.' He looked down at his brocade dressing gown. 'I'd better go and get ready. I can hardly meet Archie dressed in this.'

'Then I'll tell Leela she can clear away when we've finished our eggs.'

Breakfast over, de Silva hurriedly donned his uniform. In the hall, Bella got out of her basket and came over to rub herself against his legs. He bent down to stroke her glossy black fur. It was a pity he'd have to disappoint her today. She loved to come with him into the garden, and her playful curiosity as she explored always made him smile. Any rustling and swaying amongst the giant, elephant-eared leaves of his rhubarb patch, or in the dense greenery of the flower borders, usually meant that she was about to emerge from some adventure. His only worry was that one day she might flush out something more dangerous than frogs and toads, but Jane assured him that cats had a strong instinct for self-preservation.

'On your own?' he asked. 'Where's that brother of yours got to? Not up to mischief, I hope.'

Bella miaowed, and he smiled. 'I'll take that as a yes.'

There was the sound of a car engine on the drive. He called goodbye to Jane and went to open the front door. Archie was driving himself in the rather elderly Hillman estate that de Silva had occasionally seen him use. He looked a good deal less smart than he had the previous day, in well-worn khaki trousers and jacket with a red and white check flannel shirt.

'Mrs Clutterbuck has the official car taking her to church this morning,' he said when de Silva went out to join him. 'This will do a better job anyway. From what I remember of the Moncrieff place, the way up there's pretty rough and ready.'

He gestured to the pile of waterproof clothing on the passenger seat. 'Just toss that lot in the back.'

De Silva did so, where it joined various items of fishing tackle and a battered hat with olive-green and rust-red fishing flies tucked in the hatband. He was surprised that there was no sign of Darcy. Perhaps Archie had decided it was unwise to bring him in case Caesar was present.

'I think it will just be this medic fellow up there to meet us.' Archie raised his voice to be heard over the rattle of the Hillman's engine. 'He was the one who telephoned me this morning. Perera seems to have delegated responsibility for the affair to him. I expect Perera's still in his suite at the Crown, sleeping off the effects of celebrating his victory.'

'Is there still no news of Marina Moncrieff?'

'No. This medic fellow thinks she must be away.'

They soon left the town behind. On either side of the road, the green vista of the tea terraces that cloaked the gently rolling hills sparkled in the morning sun. A few fluffy clouds drifted across the periwinkle-blue sky.

'Splendid day yesterday,' remarked Archie. 'Good to keep up traditions. Especially at a time like this.'

De Silva took it that he meant the war.

'Doubled my money too,' Archie went on. 'Just as well, or Mrs Clutterbuck would have had something to say about the folly of gambling.' He swerved to avoid a pothole and drove on in silence. De Silva knew him well enough to realise that he was thinking carefully about how to frame his next remarks.

'I promised to tell you more about Donald Moncrieff,' he said eventually. 'His father, Victor, came out to Ceylon as a young man and bought the tea plantation we're going to. When Victor died, Donald inherited. He and his wife, Marina, were already married. Good-looking woman. She must be in her thirties by now. If I remember rightly, he's older than her by about fifteen years.'

'Do I take it that they've separated?'

'I'll come to that.'

Archie pulled out to pass a bullock cart that had been lumbering along the road in front of them for the past few minutes. 'By all accounts,' he resumed when he had completed the manoeuvre, 'Moncrieff wasn't much of a success as a tea planter. His real interest lay in racing fast cars.'

Strange, thought de Silva. He hadn't noticed the name Moncrieff among the drivers yesterday. If the man was a car enthusiast, wouldn't it be natural for him to participate in the Nuala rally?

'I expect you're wondering why he didn't race yesterday,' Archie went on. 'He didn't enter the previous rally in 1936 either, but he did take part in the 1932 event. Did pretty well as I recall, driving a Bugatti.'

'Is there any particular reason why he missed the rally this year?'

Archie squinted into the sun, frowning. 'Fact is, he disappeared shortly after the 1932 rally and no one's heard of him since.'

'Not even his wife?'

'Not a word. She's as much in the dark as anyone.'

'So, who has been running the plantation?'

'She has a manager, and from what I hear the place ticks over, although Moncrieff didn't leave it in good shape.'

Absorbing the information, de Silva felt a rush of annoyance. He had been in Nuala in 1932, admittedly new to the job, but then as now, the head of the local police.

Surely, he should at least have been informed of such an abrupt and mysterious disappearance.

'What inquiries were made about Mr Moncrieff's disappearance at the time?' he asked.

A flush crept up Archie's neck, and a furrow appeared between his eyebrows. He made a great business of edging out to try to pass another bullock cart, but there was a car coming in the other direction and he fell back. 'I decided not many were necessary,' he said at last. 'Moncrieff's other interest, aside from cars, was in the ladies – if you take my meaning. Apparently, he wasn't averse to a bit of dalliance.'

'Do you think his wife was aware of that?'

'I'm not sure, but there was always a fair amount of gossip. Around the time of the 1932 event there were rumours that the latest one was more serious than usual. When Moncrieff disappeared, it stood to reason that they'd absconded together.'

Stood to reason? On the basis of rumours, was that a deduction that could be made beyond all reasonable doubt? De Silva thought not, but he didn't comment. He waited for Archie to speak again, but the silence lengthened so eventually he decided to be the one to break it.

'If the plantation wasn't successful, how did Donald Moncrieff manage to indulge his passion for fast cars?'

Archie shrugged. 'I presume there was other family money.'

'Did his wife say anything about that at the time he disappeared?'

'No. She claimed he always kept financial matters close to his chest, but at the rate he spent on cars, and allegedly these lady friends, it must have been considerable. Victor Moncrieff, the father, married again after Donald's mother died. According to Mrs Clutterbuck, the lady in question lives in some style too.'

'Does she live in Nuala?'

'Yes, in a house on the plantation. Her name's Isobel. She never married again after Victor died.'

Archie wound down his window and ran a finger between his neck and the collar of his shirt as if he felt the heat. He speeded up a little.

'You say there were rumours that Donald Moncrieff was seeing a lady with whom it was presumed he later absconded,' said de Silva. 'Could you tell me more about these rumours? Was it ever ascertained where they originated?'

No answer. With the increased noise in the car, de Silva wondered if Archie had heard him. Either that, or he was suspiciously forgetful. He raised his voice and repeated the question.

'I heard you the first time, de Silva,' his boss said testily. 'I forget the exact circumstances. I believe there were people who backed up the story. Eight years is a long time.'

There was another pause. 'I may have kept my notes,' he added grudgingly. 'I'll see what I can look out. I do recall Moncrieff's stepmother, Isobel, telling me that she'd given up all hope of talking sense into him. She'd tried on many occasions, but he refused to mend his ways. She was convinced he'd run off with someone, and her attitude was one of good riddance. The wife was in no hurry to find him either. She didn't have much to say, but I gathered from Isobel that in addition to being unfaithful, he bullied her, and she was better off without him. In fact, he had a talent for getting up other people's noses, and very publicly too. I remember an incident at a formal dinner my wife and I gave after the 1932 rally that involved Moncrieff and yesterday's winner, Perera, who by the way seems a thoroughly decent chap. He said something complimentary about Moncrieff's Bugatti and, half joking, made him an offer for it. Instead of answering in kind, Moncrieff was churlish to the point of being insulting. Probably because Perera is a native Ceylonese. I could see Perera was extremely annoyed.'

Once more, Archie eased his collar with a finger then cast de Silva a sideways glance. 'Going back to the family, why wash the dirty linen in public and cause more distress, eh?'

And why not keep your new chief of police's nose out of the matter into the bargain? Clearly, as head of the British community, Archie had chosen to avoid a formal missing person investigation that might have caused a scandal and embarrassed the British.

'I'm sure no one would want to cause unnecessary distress, sir, but all the same, I'd be glad if you would look out your notes.'

Archie scowled. 'Are you jumping to conclusions, de Silva? Just because some remains have been found at the plantation, it doesn't prove a mistake was made in Moncrieff's case. It could be anyone. This medic chap may even have got the wrong end of the stick. It might turn out these are the bones of some animal one of the servants butchered for their own use then buried.'

From what he'd heard so far, reflected de Silva, that seemed unlikely, but he restrained himself from saying so. Annoyed as he was, he decided it was best not to be openly critical. Archie usually responded better to suggestions, especially if they were framed in a way that allowed him to think the ideas were his own.

'I merely suggest that we don't rule out anything at present, sir.'

'Damn and blast!'

The car rounded a bend and narrowly avoided an old truck that had overturned in the middle of the road. Archie slammed on the brakes and the Hillman jolted to a stop. Most of the truck's load, including numerous wooden crates, was scattered in their path. Some of the crates had broken open disgorging their cargo of chickens. In a flurry of dust and squawking, the creatures were frantically running in all directions. With little success, two men, presumably the truck driver and his companion, were trying to round them up.

'You'd better get out and take charge, de Silva,' said Archie. 'Or we'll be here all day.'

As he climbed out of the car and went to join the fray, de Silva guessed that his boss was glad of the distraction.

The Kandy road was a busy one, even on a Sunday, and soon several other trucks and carts had joined in the traffic jam. De Silva organised their drivers into a more effective chicken capturing party, and twenty minutes later the fowls had been deprived of their freedom once more and replaced in their crates where they poked their beady-eyed heads through the crooked wooden bars, clucking in incensed tones.

After the rest of the truck's cargo had been reloaded and roped down more securely than it had originally been, he went back to the Hillman and climbed in. Archie made to set off, but with a jerk, the Hillman stalled. De Silva heard another muttered expletive as his boss turned the engine on again, this time getting into first gear without mishap. They drove on for a few minutes before he ventured his next question.

'Were statements taken from the Moncrieffs' servants at the time of the disappearance?'

Archie growled something incomprehensible.

'They may have seen Donald Moncrieff with a lady,' de Silva persisted. 'They might even have overheard them making plans.' Sadly, it was not uncommon for certain types of Britisher to view their Ceylonese staff as no more sentient than the furniture in their comfortable colonial homes.

'Look, de Silva.' Archie cleared his throat. 'You may as well come out and say what you're obviously thinking. In hindsight, I accept it might have been advisable to be more thorough, but at the time I did what I thought was right.'

'I appreciate that, sir. And more searching inquiries might not have produced a different result, but I think we need to be aware that Mr Moncrieff may not have left Nuala after all. With or without a companion.'

Archie grunted. 'If you think it's necessary, we'll have to look at reopening the matter. The Moncrieffs never took much part in Nuala society,' he continued after another pause. 'I expect most people forgot about the whole business, if they'd even been aware of it in the first place. I presume that these days Marina Moncrieff spends her time at the plantation. Mrs Clutterbuck tells me that she never comes across her at social events. These days the stepmother keeps to herself too.'

He raised an eyebrow. 'I do remember that Isobel Moncrieff is a formidable lady. Before she went into her self-imposed retreat, she had a reputation for not suffering fools gladly. This morning my wife reminded me of an occasion at a garden party at the Residence where a junior member of my staff had the bad luck to spill a drink and splash her dress. She skewered him with such an arctic look that the poor fellow was a gibbering wreck for the rest of the afternoon.'

De Silva didn't comment. It still rankled that he had been passed over. He wondered if the same thing would happen today if something came up that Archie would prefer to keep quiet. He hoped not, and that his eight years in Nuala would prove that he knew how to handle sensitive situations with discretion. He glanced at Archie and was surprised to see that the expression on his face might reasonably be described as apologetic.

'I know, I know. With hindsight, the matter could have been better handled.'

It was the nearest de Silva reckoned Archie would get to an apology, and it clearly wasn't easy for him.

'Very few people can look back and think that there's nothing in their lives they would have done differently,' de Silva said, slightly mollified.

'Thank you. I'm loath to open a can of worms, but if it seems unavoidable, naturally I'll support you.'

'That's good of you, sir.'

Archie frowned. 'But I'll want some pretty persuasive evidence that it's the case,' he added.

'Of course.'

'I'm not keen to dredge up things that are best forgotten.' He slowed the car and turned onto a narrow track. 'Almost there. Hopefully, this will turn out to be a storm in a teacup and we can be on our way back to town in no time. I don't know about you, de Silva, but this wasn't the way I intended to spend my Sunday.'

* * *

They drove up to the front door of a house that didn't quite match the Residence in size but was nonetheless a large one. It was for the most part built in the Portuguese style. De Silva noticed that the paint on the window frames had worn in many places, revealing dry, cracked wood underneath. The whitewashed walls would have benefited from a coat of paint and there were several places on the roof where tiles had slipped or broken. From what he could see of the garden, it looked as if no one took much interest in it.

A car was already on the drive. Its driver got out and came over to greet them. 'Good morning.' He held out a hand to shake Archie's. 'I take it you're Mr Clutterbuck.'

'Yes, and this is Inspector de Silva, our local chief of police.'

The man gave de Silva a nod. 'I'm Doctor Michael Rudd. Johnny Perera asked me to deal with this nasty business. He was extremely shocked by what we found.'

De Silva wondered whether Rudd really believed that it was shock that made Perera want to stay away. He doubted that a man like him, who presumably had the nerves of steel needed to drive in the Nuala rally, would be overwhelmed by the discovery of some old bones. More likely he was just accustomed to having someone else to do anything he found uncongenial or inconvenient. A comfortable bed and an excellent breakfast at the Crown were probably far more appealing than an excursion back to the plantation. The next minute, however, he reprimanded himself for the ungenerous thought. Being a racing driver didn't inevitably render a man insensitive. In view of the risks he ran, Perera might have a horror of being reminded of death.

Archie's voice intruded on his thoughts. 'Well, I suppose we'd better get on with what we came here for. Will you show the way, Rudd?'

They set off along a path that took them around the left-hand side of the building. It led to a courtyard where weeds sprouted from the cracks between the stone flags. There were garages on three sides of it. The doors of one were open. At first, after the brightness of the sunshine outside, de Silva found it hard to see what it contained, but when his eyes became accustomed to the gloom, he noticed that there was an inspection pit at one end, and a variety of automobile spare parts were shelved around the walls.

'Did Mr Perera have a particular reason for wanting to come up here last night?' he asked. 'Was he looking for something?'

Rudd paused and turned to him. 'Nothing specific, but I think he hoped that at least one of Donald Moncrieff's racing cars might still be here; it's well known that he amassed a good collection, in particular a Bugatti. And as I told Mr Clutterbuck, Johnny also wanted to revisit the place for old times' sake.'

'How long has it been since he lived here?'

Rudd thought for a moment before answering. 'It must be around twenty years since his father sold the place. Johnny told me he was in his mid-teens.' De Silva noted the absence of any explanation of how Perera had got into the garage.

'It was when we were inside here that we noticed Johnny's dog Caesar wasn't with us. Then we heard this furious barking from beyond the garages. Caesar must have gone off to explore by himself as we came into the court-yard. Johnny was concerned he would wake up the servants, if not the current owner, so we hurried towards the barking with a view to calming Caesar down and making our escape pretty smartish. That's when we found the remains. Come, gentlemen, I'll show you the way.'

'As far as you're aware, was last night the first time Mr Perera's been back?' asked de Silva as he and Archie followed Rudd into the sunshine.

'I think so.'

'Did he explain why the family left?'

'Yes. Apparently, his father was in the tea business for a while before he changed to growing rubber. There was no point in keeping the plantation, so he sold up to Victor Moncrieff, Donald's father.'

'Did you find any cars in any of the other garages?' asked Archie.

Rudd shook his head. 'We had a mosey around the place but all we found were spare parts, although the photographs pinned up in various places bore out that Moncrieff had owned a pretty impressive collection over the years.'

While Archie and Rudd walked ahead of him, Archie asking the medic questions about the cars, de Silva reflected that if Rudd was right about this being the first time Perera had chosen to visit his old home, it was strange. It wasn't the first time he'd been back to Nuala. He'd taken part in the previous two rallies and maybe more. Why this sudden desire to come up to the plantation? Was it simply a matter of getting older? A yearning for times gone by? But then again, Perera was still a relatively young man.

The path in the overgrown area they were walking through was hard to discern and the going was rough. Temporarily, the need to watch where he put his feet distracted de Silva from speculating any further. All around them trees furred with damp moss and heavy with vines and lianas reached for the sky, blotting out the sunshine and leaving only murky grey-green light. Steamy air soon had de Silva's face filmed with sweat; he felt his shirt stick to his skin. Underfoot, dry, leathery leaves crackled and twigs snapped. Thorny bushes caught on his clothes, and roots snagged his feet. Once, when they had to scramble over fallen tree trunks, he saw the slimy black shapes of some leeches in the crevices of the gnarled bark. Instinctively, he reached for his wrinkled socks and yanked them up to his knees.

At last they came to a clearing. Ahead, he saw a place where the ground fell away sharply to a gully. Uprooted bushes and small trees, and the trails of rocks and pebbles that littered the slope, indicated there had been a landslide. Very likely one of the heavy monsoon rainstorms had been responsible.

At the sight of de Silva and his companions, the three men sitting on the brow of the slope scrambled to their feet and stood to attention. A tarpaulin was spread out on the ground a few yards in front of them.

'They're servants from the plantation,' said Rudd. 'Last night we found them asleep in one of the outhouses and got them down here to help with the digging. I didn't like to remove the bones we unearthed, so I instructed them to keep watch in case there were wild animals about.'

De Silva felt sympathy for the three men. All they seemed to have by way of protection were the spades they must have used for digging and a couple of oil lanterns. They would have been of limited use if a hungry leopard came along. He doubted that the rough ground had provided a comfortable resting place either.

Rudd slithered a little way down the slope and pulled the tarpaulin aside to reveal a shallow trench. Peering into it, de Silva saw that a jumble of bones, including a skull, lay in it. Some of the bones were half embedded in the red earth, others fully disinterred. Indubitably, they were human.

'The deceased was male,' said Rudd, regaining the brow of the slope and dusting off his hands on his khaki trouser legs. 'At least six foot, I'd say.'

'Not much to go on,' remarked Archie with a frown.

'I'm afraid not, but I did notice something that may help you. The tibia, or shinbone, of the left leg had been broken in two places. The bone had been reset with considerable skill and looks to have healed very satisfactorily. One can always tell where new tissue has knit bone together. In my opinion, we are not looking at the remains of a local villager. More likely someone with access to sophisticated medical care from a specialist surgeon. Perhaps the local surgery or hospital will have information that helps you to identify the deceased.'

'Hmm, interesting. It's worth a few enquiries. D'you agree, de Silva?'

De Silva nodded.

'Have a word with Doctor Hebden when we get back to town. See if he remembers treating an injury like that.'

'Very well, sir.' If Hebden did, and the patient had been Donald Moncrieff, the first question this mystery threw up would be solved.

'Anything else that might help us, Rudd?'

'Not as far as I can tell. If he was clothed when he was buried, the clothes have rotted away, and if he wore a watch or anything made of metal, a ring for example, whoever buried him must have removed it first.'

'Any idea how long he's been here?' asked Archie.

'Hard to say. In a tropical climate, skeletonization tends to occur relatively quickly, often within a year of death, especially where plentiful insect life is present in the soil. Final disintegration, however, takes much longer, probably up to twenty years. So, take your choice of somewhere between the two.'

'Any indication of the cause of death that you've noticed?'

Rudd shrugged. 'Nothing jumps out.'

From the furrow that appeared between Archie's eyebrows, de Silva wondered if he was finding Rudd's dismissive manner irritating too, but if he was, he kept it to himself.

'Anything more you want to look at, de Silva?' he asked, stirring the dusty ground with his stick.

More for the sake of form than in the hope of any great revelations, de Silva picked his way down the slope to the shallow trench and hunkered down next to it. He picked up a flat, sharp-edged stone that lay near the bones and poked about with it for a few moments before straightening up and scrambling back to level ground. 'I'll send my sergeant and my constable up here later to make a search of the surrounding area, but for the moment, I agree that unless something new comes to light from another source, the broken leg gives us our best chance of finding out who this was.'

'Do you think there's been foul play?' asked Rudd.

'I think it's very likely. If this man had been a Christian, he wouldn't legitimately have been buried out here. Equally, cremation is the most common way for Buddhists and Hindus to dispose of their dead.'

'What if he was Muslim?' asked Archie.

'I've had some experience of Muslim funeral practices

when I was working in Egypt,' Rudd interjected before de Silva had time to answer. 'Cremation is forbidden, but it's customary to bury the dead in cemeteries.'

'Isn't there some ancient custom of forest burial, de Silva?' asked Archie.

Now he was clutching at straws, thought de Silva. 'Yes sir,' he said patiently. 'It's true there's an old tradition whereby the body of the deceased is wrapped in a white cloth and a sleeping mat, then taken deep into the jungle and left there to be consumed by animals.' He looked around him at the spindly fallen trees and scrubby ground. 'But I'd hardly describe this area as deep jungle, and I doubt anyone would perform a forest burial so close to habitation, particularly on British property. Also the expensive work done on the broken leg suggests that this was not someone whom one would expect to have a forest burial. I'm pretty sure this man was murdered, and his killer buried the body out here hoping it would never be found.'

Archie studied his shoes. 'You may be right,' he muttered.

There was an awkward pause, broken by Michael Rudd. 'If there's nothing more I can do, I'll be on my way.' He looked rather bored now. *Probably keen to get back to the comfort of the Crown Hotel*, thought de Silva.

'Of course,' said Archie. 'Thank you for your help. Unpleasant business. I hope it hasn't taken the shine off your man's victory yesterday.'

Rudd smiled. 'Oh, I think Johnny will rise above it. Well, I'll be on my way.'

'Decent enough fellow,' remarked Archie as Rudd disappeared into the trees. 'What do you want to do next, de Silva?'

'I'd like a word with these men.' He gestured to the three servants who stood a little way off looking increasingly gloomy. 'Once I've done that, I suggest we leave them here on guard and go back up to the house. We need something to transport the bones in. The ground's far too rough for the undertakers to drive down here. I'll call them and ask them to collect from there then they can keep the bones safe until we can arrange a proper burial.'

'Quite right. Whoever this fellow was, his remains ought to be treated with respect.'

De Silva went over to the servants and spoke to them.

'We do not know anything, sahib,' the eldest man said nervously. 'We told the doctor sahib and his friends this already. We were sleeping when they woke us to come and dig. We did not know what we would find.'

De Silva nodded. 'I see, and how long have you worked here?'

'For five years, sahib.'

De Silva looked at the other men. 'And what about you?'

They mumbled they had worked at the plantation for three and five years respectively.

So, none of them had been employed in Donald Moncrieff's time.

'I want you to stay here for a while longer,' he said. 'The sahib and I will send something you can move these bones on. I want them brought up to the house.'

The eldest man looked worried.

'I'll come here again to help you,' de Silva said quickly. 'I don't expect you to carry out the operation on your own.'

'Yes, sahib. Thank you, sahib.'

'Once you've dealt with the bones,' said Archie as they retraced their steps in the direction of the house, 'I suggest we find out where Marina Moncrieff is and speak with her. Whatever the outcome, and her history with her husband, she may well be distressed by all this. We'll have to tread carefully. With luck, there'll be some woman friend who can be called to sit with her. After that, we should call the rest of the servants together. I hope we can find out whether any of them recall any disappearances, unexplained or otherwise, from amongst their number. I'm wondering if there was ever bad blood between any of them, and a murder went undiscovered or was hushed up.'

De Silva gave him a sideways glance. He wasn't prepared to let his boss off the hook as easily as all that. Archie looked a little crestfallen.

'I agree that we should speak with Marina Moncrieff as soon as possible, sir. As the remains have been found on her property, she ought to be informed. But I'll be surprised if this can be put down to a quarrel between servants.'

Archie didn't reply.

CHAPTER 3

Back at the house, a servant opened the front door to them. He eyed Archie and de Silva cautiously. 'How can I help you, sahibs?'

'Is Mrs Marina Moncrieff here? We need to speak with her as a matter of urgency.'

The man looked apologetic. 'I think she is not at home. She did not order breakfast this morning, but if you will wait, please, I will see what I can find out for you.'

He left them standing on the doorstep and disappeared inside.

'Odd,' remarked Archie. 'You'd think a servant would know where the mistress of the house is. If she's away, why doesn't he say so?'

Several minutes passed. Irritably, Archie flicked away a fly that buzzed around him. 'Dratted thing! What on earth's this fellow up to keeping us waiting out here like this? Either she's here or she's not.'

That was an unarguable conclusion, thought de Silva, but he said nothing. Archie took a step into the gloomy hall and almost collided with a new man who was more smartly dressed than the porter.

'I am sorry you have been kept waiting, sahibs. I understand you asked to see the memsahib, but she is out.'

'Do you know where she is?' asked de Silva.

The man shook his head. 'When I saw her yesterday, she

did not mention she would be going out, but today her car is not here.'

'Who saw her last?'

'Her maid, Prema.'

'When was that?'

'After dinner last night. The memsahib said she did not need her for the rest of the evening. She wanted to read in her bedroom. Prema was to tell one of the other servants to lock up and then go to her quarters.'

'Is there a nightwatchman?'

'Yes, but he does not sleep in the main building. In the morning, when Prema took the memsahib her tea as usual, she was not there, and her bed had not been slept in.'

De Silva frowned. It sounded as if security arrangements at the Moncrieffs' establishment were somewhat lax. 'Thank you. And what is your name?'

'Muttu. I am the head of the servants here. Is there some problem, sahib?'

'Yes, the skeleton of a man has been found in the wooded area behind the garage courtyard.'

Muttu's eyes widened. 'You are sure, sahib?'

'Of course we're sure,' said Archie testily. 'Has anyone been reported missing since you started work here?'

A guarded look came over Muttu's face. De Silva wondered how much he knew about the history of the Moncrieff family.

'No one is accusing you or any of the other servants of anything,' de Silva said patiently. 'But last night, a gentleman by the name of Perera and his friends came here. Mr Perera once lived at the plantation, and he wished to revisit his old home. If Mrs Moncrieff was here, she didn't come out to meet them. One of them had a dog with him. A large and powerful dog. It dug up some bones in the area behind the garage courtyard. A place where there looks to have been a landslide quite recently.'

Muttu looked puzzled. 'I know the place you mean, sahib, but no one goes there. The ground is too poor to grow vegetables. It is not good for anything.'

'Nevertheless, someone buried a man's body there, but we aren't sure when. Some of Mr Perera's friends called three of your staff to do some digging, and they found the skeleton. If anyone on this plantation knows who the man was, it's imperative they keep nothing back. Do you understand?'

'Yes, sahib. Shall I tell them you wish to speak with them?'

'All in good time. First, we need a conveyance of some kind to transport the bones back here. Some sacking would be useful too. To protect them.'

Muttu looked relieved at the prospect of having something to do. 'Right away, sahib.'

'And find someone to take it down to where we found the bones. I can show him the way.'

'I'll be glad to leave that to you, de Silva,' said Archie, mopping his forehead. 'Dashed hot this morning. If there's somewhere handy in the shade, I'll park myself and wait for you to get back.'

'Very well, sir.'

Muttu returned with another servant who was pushing a wooden barrow, the kind of thing that de Silva kept for use in his garden. It didn't seem the most respectful of conveyances, but anything bigger would probably not be able to negotiate the rough track successfully.

'I hope this will do, sahib,' said Muttu.

De Silva nodded. 'The sahib will stay here. Please find him somewhere to sit where he can be cool.'

'The drawing room is cool. Shall I bring something to drink?'

De Silva saw Archie cast a surreptitious glance at his wristwatch. No doubt in his present state, he would welcome a whisky, but it was rather early for that.

'Sun's not over the yardarm yet,' he said gruffly. 'Better make it a cup of tea.'

Leaving the servant to show Archie the way to the drawing room, de Silva led the man with the barrow back to the place where the bones had been found. As he walked, he wondered where Marina Moncrieff had got to. Had she been reading in her room the previous evening, as she had told her maid she planned to? Maybe she had been wary about coming out to face a crowd of strangers. She might even have been afraid that the place was about to be broken into. But if that was the case, why not call for help? Particularly where isolated properties were concerned, most owners had a telephone, or if not, at least some kind of system rigged up to enable them to raise the alarm if they feared there was danger. He had heard of people using bells or firecrackers to scare unwelcome visitors away. They were also useful as deterrents against marauding elephants. He supposed it was possible that Marina Moncrieff had heard intruders and been too frightened to act. Or was she a deep sleeper and unaware that she had unexpected visitors? But her bed had not been slept in.

The only other explanation he could think of was that she hadn't actually been in residence when Perera and his friends arrived. He remembered Rudd telling Archie that they hadn't found any cars in the garages, and if she had fled to escape supposed intruders wouldn't Rudd have heard her car engine as she left? Whatever the case, it was odd that she had absented herself without telling her servants when to expect her back.

He arrived at the site of the shallow grave, the servant with the barrow trundling along behind, and the three servants jumped to attention. Under de Silva's direction, they and the barrow pusher lifted the bones and placed them carefully on a bed of sacking. When de Silva was satisfied that nothing had been missed, they returned to the house.

Muttu was waiting for them in the forecourt.

'You'd better find a safe place to stow these until I have time to send the undertakers up to collect them,' said de Silva. 'But first, show me to the drawing room.'

In the drawing room, Archie looked up at his entrance. There was a half-finished cup of tea on the table at his elbow and a crumpled newspaper by his feet.

'Weeks old,' he said. 'Things look to be slack around here. Anything new to report?'

'No, except for the fact the bones are up here now. When we get back to town, I'll speak with the undertakers about collecting them, but before we leave, I think we ought to call the staff together. When Muttu returns from finding somewhere safe for the bones, I'll tell him to organise it.'

Archie stood up and went to one of the tall windows. De Silva joined him. The morning sun shone in, casting a pool of buttery light on the faded Indian rug that covered part of the parquet floor. Archie appeared to be scrutinising the view of the neglected garden with considerable intensity.

'A pity the place hasn't been better cared for,' he remarked. 'Marina Moncrieff would probably have done better to cut her losses and move on. But perhaps the property's still in Moncrieff's name. I can see that would be problematic.'

De Silva dredged his memory for the legal principle he had learnt for the law paper in his police examinations. 'If a person has not been heard of for seven years, I believe that a ruling may be obtained from the courts that they have died.'

'Presumption of death,' said Archie nodding. 'But I think there's a bit more to it than that. A judge would need to be satisfied that proper inquiries and attempts to find the person had been made. We've no information as to whether that's been done.'

He continued to look out at the garden. A flock of parrots had just descended on a climbing passion fruit plant that smothered a dilapidated arbour at the far side of the unkempt patch of lawn. With powerful beaks, they began to strip the fruit.

There was the sound of footsteps on the parquet floor. De Silva turned and saw that a tall, lean European man had joined them. Tanned, with fair hair and blue eyes, he exuded the air of someone who lived the outdoor life.

'Good morning, gentlemen. Can I help you?'

Archie surveyed him. 'And you are?'

'Flint. Peter Flint. I run the plantation for Marina Moncrieff.'

'Then perhaps you can tell us where she's got to. Her staff seem to have no idea.'

Flint frowned. 'That's strange. She doesn't usually go far apart from the occasional shopping trip to Hatton, but that's not likely as it's a Sunday. She doesn't keep up with many friends these days, but if she has gone visiting, I think she would have told one of the servants.'

'Do you usually come up here on a Sunday morning, Mr Flint?' asked de Silva.

'Not often, but Marina contacted me to say she was having trouble with her car. It wouldn't start and could I help. I was busy yesterday afternoon, so I said I'd look in this morning if there was still a problem. I was pretty sure it was just that she'd flooded the engine. She has a habit of over-choking it. This morning I didn't hear from her, so I assumed the problem had sorted itself out, but I decided to come up anyway. She sounded very low yesterday. I'm afraid that she suffers from bouts of depression.'

Flint broke off and his frown deepened. 'Look, you ask a lot of questions, but you haven't told me who you are, or more to the point, what you're doing here.'

Archie's eyes glinted; he drew himself up to his full height. 'Archibald Clutterbuck, Assistant Government Agent for the Nuala district.'

Peter Flint had the grace to look slightly embarrassed. 'My apologies, I didn't recognise you.'

COLD CASE IN NUALA

'And this is my Chief of Police, Inspector de Silva.'

Flint nodded to de Silva and murmured an acknowledgment.

'We're here to investigate an incident that was reported early this morning,' Archie went on. 'Last night, the skeleton of a man was discovered buried on this property.'

'What? Where and by whom?'

'You explain, de Silva.'

Flint listened as de Silva explained about the visit of Perera and his friends and the circumstances that led to the discovery of the bones. For the moment, he didn't voice his suspicion that they belonged to Donald Moncrieff. As he talked, he studied Flint's expression but was unable to detect anything except concern and surprise. On the face of it, the whole business came as news to the manager. 'We came up here hoping to find Mrs Moncrieff,' he concluded. 'She ought to be informed. She may even be able to throw some light on the affair.'

'Now steady on,' Flint said warily. 'Marina wouldn't hide something like this. You say the grave is in the area behind the garages. To the best of my knowledge, no one ever goes there, and it's not been used for anything in my time. Anyone looking for a place to bury an inconvenient body might have trespassed on the property and found the spot.'

'Unlikely,' said Archie. 'Given this plantation's isolation, I doubt anyone would do that unless they already knew it existed.'

'Are you suggesting some of the servants are involved?' asked Flint. 'Do you want to question them?'

'Yes. Muttu, who met us when we arrived, is finding a safe place for the bones but he should be back here soon,' said de Silva. 'We'll speak to him about it then.'

'I don't have much to do with the household staff, but I can make a similar arrangement with the plantation workers if you think it's necessary.'

'Thank you. We'll deal with them when we've spoken to the household staff. I can't stress too strongly that none of them are to let it be known that they've been questioned as that might well prejudice my inquiries.'

'Understood.' Flint hesitated. 'Have you any idea who the dead man was?'

'That's yet to be established. There is something that may help us with that, however. A doctor at the scene observed that, prior to death, the man's left tibia had been broken in two places.'

Once again, de Silva studied Peter Flint's expression carefully. 'I assume you're aware of Donald Moncrieff's racing career. Do you have any idea whether he suffered an injury to his left leg at any time?'

'I don't recall it being mentioned. I came here in '28 when his father, Victor, was in failing health and unable to cope with the day-to-day running of the business. When he died two years later, Donald inherited, but I never knew him well. He didn't spend a lot of time here. As you may know, he left Nuala years ago and hasn't been heard from since.'

'How would you describe his relationship with his wife, Marina?'

'I didn't often see them together, but from what I observed and heard from other people, it wasn't a happy one. Isobel, his stepmother, often said she believed that Marina was far better off without him. For herself, Isobel certainly didn't seem to regret his disappearance. She found him difficult to deal with and irresponsible where the plantation and the rest of his inheritance from his father were concerned.'

'And how did you find him to work for?'

Flint shrugged. 'Not easy, I'm afraid. I frequently had the feeling he only disagreed with my ideas for the business for the sake of proving he was boss. His passion for racing didn't help. I tried to persuade him that taking out so much of the profit was harmful to the business, but he wasn't having any of it, and the place soon went downhill. It's taking a long time to get it back to where it should be.'

'Yet you stayed.'

Flint grimaced. 'I was looking around for another job, but then he left. Isobel and Marina needed help and wanted me to stay on. As you see, I'm still here.' He shrugged. 'One gets into a rut and sometimes it's easier to remain in it.'

Muttu came into the room. He didn't seem surprised to see Peter Flint who nodded at him. 'I hear we have an unpleasant situation.'

'Yes, sahib.' He turned to de Silva. 'The bones are safe as you ordered, sahib. What shall I do now?'

'I want you to collect the indoor and garden servants together.'

Muttu looked uncertain.

'On the forecourt will do.'

* * *

Nineteen staff including the three diggers that de Silva and Archie had already encountered awaited them on the gravel in front of the house. The low buzz of talk hushed as they emerged. De Silva presumed that the three diggers had already imparted news of the finds.

'Can you all hear me?' he began in a loud voice.

There was a murmur of assent.

'I want to know from each of you when you last saw the memsahib.'

He pointed to the man closest to him on the left. One by one, each of the servants answered the same question. As Muttu had already said, the last person to see Marina Moncrieff had been her maid and that had been early in the evening.

He went on to his next question. 'I expect you know by now that human bones have been found buried in the area behind the garages. We're not sure yet whose body this is, but if any of you know anything about it, anything at all, you must tell us. Do you understand?'

Again there was a murmur of assent, but no one stepped forward.

'Did any of you work here in the time of sahib Moncrieff?'

Only six hands went up.

'Then think back eight years to when he left the plantation.'

Studying the men who had raised their hands, de Silva estimated that at least two of them would have been in their teens then, but perhaps the older ones would have taken an interest in the goings-on of the Britishers and remembered something useful. 'What do you remember about that time? Was there anything that made you think the sahib might leave? Or did you have any reason to think someone wanted to harm him?'

He waited, surveying faces whose expressions ranged from blank to suspicious. He feared this was going to get him nowhere, but he had to try. There was a chance one of these people had overheard a conversation or seen something that might shed light on what really happened all those years ago.

'You need not say anything now,' he said after a minute had passed. 'If you have something to tell me, you may do so in private. Speak to Muttu and he will arrange it. One last thing: there is to be no talk about this meeting to anyone who was not here and if there is, the culprit will be in serious trouble.'

'Shall I dismiss them, sahib?' asked Muttu.

De Silva glanced at Archie. 'May as well,' Archie grunted. 'No help there.' As the servants dispersed, he turned to Muttu. 'Any sign of the lady's car yet?'

'No, sahib. Do you need me for something else, sahib?'

Archie shook his head. 'I think that will do for the moment, don't you agree, de Silva?'

'Do you still want to speak to the plantation staff?' asked Flint as Muttu disappeared into the house.

'No harm I suppose,' said Archie. 'But we'll keep it short, eh, de Silva?'

'The main drying shed should be the best place,' said Flint. 'There's no work going on there today. It's too far to walk, so if you gentlemen would like to come in your car, I'll lead the way.'

*   *   *

The air in the main drying shed was perfumed with the aroma of tea. In the half-light filtering through the small windows, de Silva saw a cavernous, low-roofed space that contained five rows of long metal troughs. Whatever Flint said about Donald Moncrieff's bad management, the operation didn't look too shabby now, presumably thanks to Flint.

'If you'll wait here,' he said, 'I'll fetch the workers.'

After Flint left them, Archie ambled between the rows of troughs, apparently deep in thought. De Silva left him alone for a while then went to join him.

'It occurs to me, sir, that it would be strange if Donald Moncrieff didn't have some of his money in a Ceylon bank. What happened to it may give us a lead. Would you make enquiries? I think a request for information might come better from you than from me.'

Archie rubbed his chin. 'Hmm, good point. I suppose I could make a few calls and see what I can find out.' He looked a little sheepish. 'Unfortunately, quite a few years have passed.'

'There's still a chance that we might be able to establish where the money ended up,' said de Silva tactfully.

Archie raised an eyebrow. 'You mean if Moncrieff's not spending it, who is?'

'Exactly, sir.'

Peter Flint reappeared, bringing a group of women and a smaller one of men with him. It was a common division of labour on tea estates. With their nimbler fingers, the women did the more labour-intensive plucking of the leaves and sorting of the tips that were used to make tea, while men did the packing and lifting. The workers looked nervous, and he did his best to reassure them that they were in no trouble. It didn't take long, however, to establish that there was even less chance of enlightenment here than there had been with the domestic staff.

'Much obliged for your help, Flint,' said Archie as the workers filed out of the shed.

'I'm afraid it didn't amount to much.'

'Can't be helped. So, the question of Marina Moncrieff's whereabouts is still up in the air.'

'I'm sure there'll be an innocent explanation for where she's gone,' Flint said firmly. 'I can't believe she had anything to do with this business.'

'All the same, when she returns, I want you to contact me or Inspector de Silva immediately.'

They left Flint at the plantation and returned to the house.

'You'd better circulate a description of Marina Moncrieff,' said Archie on the way. 'Hopefully, there'll be a suitable photograph at the house that you can use. If she's travelling alone, that would be quite unusual for a British lady and someone may spot her.'

'I'll do that, sir, and I'd like to have a look around the place generally. There may be something that provides a clue as to her whereabouts.'

When they rang the bell, Muttu answered the door and let them in. He followed them from room to room as they opened drawers and cupboards. They found nothing in the way of business correspondence or other paperwork; everything appertaining to the running of the plantation must be kept elsewhere. From what he saw, de Silva got the impression that either Marina Moncrieff lived very quietly, or she never kept anything. There were no private papers or letters, only a few receipted bills for supplies of household essentials and for occasional purchases of clothes and shoes from the ladies' shops in Hatton. Entries in a notebook recorded the names of the inside and outside staff and the dates and amounts of the wages they were paid.

The furniture in the main rooms looked to be of good quality, but there were very few ornaments or pictures to give the place a personal touch and an air of comfort. The books on the shelves were a random collection of historical novels, mysteries, and romances. De Silva ran his finger along the tops of the volumes, and it came away with a light coating of dust. If Marina Moncrieff had been reading the previous evening, it didn't appear to be a regular activity. By all accounts, she didn't join in with the local social activities either. From the unloved look of the house and its grounds, she wasn't interested in gardening, wasn't particularly house-proud and left the running of the plantation to Peter Flint. De Silva wondered what she did do to pass the time.

'Depressing place,' muttered Archie. 'I suppose when Moncrieff left, she lost heart.'

Or had already lost it, thought de Silva. This wasn't the house of a happily married couple.

The task of examining the bedroom accommodation didn't take long. Only the bedroom that Marina Moncrieff occupied had much in it.

'Dashed uncomfortable going through a lady's things,' Archie soon said. 'You'd better finish off, de Silva. I'll see you back in the drawing room.'

De Silva checked the last of the drawers and then the cupboards. There was nothing that he would not have expected to find. Muttu watched from the doorway as he picked up a silver-framed photograph from the dressing table. It showed a couple, presumably Donald and Marina Moncrieff standing by a silver Bugatti. Both were casually dressed and wore dark glasses. His arm was around her shoulders and they were smiling. At least there had been some happy moments. The dark glasses made the photograph less than ideal for identification purposes, but he hadn't seen a better one.

'I need to take this,' he said to Muttu. The servant nodded unwillingly.

They returned to the drawing room where Archie was waiting. 'Ah, good man, you found a photograph.' Archie studied it. 'Not the clearest likeness but it will have to do. We may as well be getting along.' He turned to Muttu. 'Do you have a telephone here?'

Muttu nodded.

'If your mistress returns, you're to call the police station, and if that's closed the Residence, straight away. Do you understand?'

'I understand, sahib. But what will I tell the memsahib?'

'Nothing. After you've done that, the inspector and I will deal with the rest.'

CHAPTER 4

Archie drove off after dropping him home to Sunnybank and de Silva let himself into the bungalow. A black furry form emerged from the shadows of the cool hallway to greet him. He bent down to pick her up. 'Hello, Bella. Are you on your own?'

She replied with a plaintive miaow. Still carrying her, he strolled into the drawing room. It was empty and there was no sign of Jane on the verandah either, although Billy was curled up asleep on her chair. He went back into the hall and called out. A moment later one of the servants appeared.

'Where is the memsahib?' de Silva asked.

'She has gone to have lunch with Doctor Hebden and Mrs Hebden, sahib. She was not sure when you would be back, but I can bring food for you if you wish.'

'Thank you, I've had no lunch and I'm ravenous. Call me when it's ready. I'll be on the verandah.'

Half an hour later, he was just finishing his solitary meal when the telephone rang. Pushing away his plate, he put his crumpled napkin on the table, got up and went into the hall.

'Have you been home for long?' asked Jane from the other end of the line.

'An hour or so. I hear you've been having lunch with the Hebdens.'

'Yes, it was a last-minute invitation. Emerald telephoned to ask if I was going to church. She wasn't feeling up to it herself but had a book she wanted returning to the vicar's wife. As I had already decided not to go, I offered to take it another time, but when I told her you'd gone out and I wasn't sure when you'd be back, she invited me over for lunch. David very kindly came to fetch me.'

'I hope there was nothing seriously wrong with Emerald.'

'On no, she just gets tired sometimes. It's not long until the baby's due. She had a rest and then was in good spirits over lunch. But tell me how you got on this morning. I hope you don't mind that I told Emerald and David where you and Archie had gone. David recalled that Marina Moncrieff came to see him several years ago. He said she was very distressed because her husband had left home without any explanation and she had no idea where he was. He prescribed some medication for her nerves and told her to come back if she needed more help, but she never did.'

'Well, it seems the husband never came back, and now Marina Moncrieff is missing too. But I'll tell you more when I see you. Shall I pick you up?'

'That would be lovely. We're just having coffee in the garden. Emerald says you must join us.'

'Excellent. I need a word with David in any case. I think the dead man may be Donald Moncrieff, and I hope he can help me to prove it.'

* * *

The Hebdens' bungalow was in the same style as Sunny-bank with a deep, shady porch to the front and a verandah running along the length of the building to the rear. The garden was, however, a different matter. David Hebden's interests lay in sport. He was particularly keen on cricket and generally recognised to be the best player in the Nuala team. He was the first to admit that where gardening was concerned, he barely knew the difference between an orchid and an onion. The bungalow's garden was kept tidy by two gardeners but when one of the house servants showed de Silva out to the verandah, as always he couldn't help thinking of what he would like to do if the place was his.

Hebden stood up to greet him. 'Good afternoon, old chap.'

De Silva kissed Jane's cheek and Emerald's proffered hand. 'How are you, dear lady?' he asked.

'I feel like a beached whale, and a very hot one at that.'

'I'm sure no whale has ever looked so lovely.'

She laughed. 'You always know the right thing to say.' She signalled to the servant who had shown de Silva through. 'Bring another cup and some fresh coffee, please. Would you like anything to eat, Shanti?'

'Thank you, but I've just had lunch.' He grinned. 'The waistline police would not approve of more.'

'Settle yourself down,' said Hebden. 'I understand you've had a busy morning.'

'Yes, as I expect Jane's told you, Archie Clutterbuck called at breakfast time and wanted me to go up to the Moncrieff plantation with him.'

'And a dead body has been discovered there.'

'Not exactly a body,' de Silva said.

He explained about Perera and his friends visiting the plantation and what they found, going on to describe his own visit with Archie. 'So, we have a suspicious burial and a vanished husband,' he finished. 'I don't think one needs to be Hercule Poirot to put two and two together and reach the conclusion that the bones in that grave may belong to Donald Moncrieff.' He looked at David Hebden. 'I hope you can help me put some flesh on that theory.'

'So, Marina Moncrieff is nowhere to be found,' said Jane thoughtfully.

'Goodness, do you think she murdered him?' asked Emerald with a frown. 'If this were a detective novel, I think it would be too simple an answer. The story would be over almost before it began.'

De Silva smiled. 'Real life doesn't necessarily follow the pattern of fiction, but I grant you that it's too soon to close off all other avenues of investigation. Nevertheless, I want to find Marina Moncrieff as soon as possible. At the moment, she has to be my prime suspect.'

The coffee arrived and he sipped his while the four of them talked and he told them more about the Moncrieff plantation, Flint, its manager, and Donald Moncrieff's stepmother, Isobel.

'She sounds a dragon,' remarked Emerald. 'And she obviously didn't care for her stepson.'

'From what Archie told me, not many people did.'

'You said you hoped I could help you to put some flesh on your theory,' said Hebden. 'What did you mean by that?'

'The man's left tibia had been broken in two places. Perera's doctor, Michael Rudd, pointed out that the break had been fixed and the bone fused before death. Do you have any memory of treating Donald Moncrieff for such a thing?'

Hebden pondered for a few moments. 'I'm afraid not. I don't recall him ever coming to me for treatment. That's not to say he didn't have an accident before my time. When Doctor Lucas retired, he left his notes on his patients at the surgery. It will take me a while to go back through them, but I'll do that and see what I can find for you.'

'I'd be most grateful.'

Emerald smothered a yawn. 'Oh, please excuse me. I seem to have no more energy than a baby at the moment.'

Jane smiled. 'I think that must have something to do with the fact that you'll soon have one.' She stood up. 'We should be going, Shanti.' She patted Emerald on the shoulder. 'Take good care of yourself, my dear. I'll telephone you in the week for a chat.'

'That would be lovely.'

'And thank you for the offer of help,' said de Silva to Hebden.

'My pleasure.'

* * *

As they drove home to Sunnybank, distant views of the green hills of the tea terraces flashed between the gaps in the trees lining the road. The taste of coffee still lingering in his mouth, de Silva wondered how different the landscape of the Hill Country would have looked if the coffee plantations that had originally cloaked the hills had not been devastated by the blight that had ruined many planters. Today, the tea grown in the ideal climate of the uplands was Ceylon's most famous and one of her most profitable crops. Donald Moncrieff must indeed have been a neglectful owner if the Moncrieff plantation had run into difficulties in a couple of years as Peter Flint claimed.

'A penny for your thoughts,' said Jane.

'I was thinking about tea. Peter Flint indicated that he's still working to make the Moncrieff plantation as profitable as it should be after Donald mismanaged it. But with all the advantages up here, I'm surprised a couple of years had such a damaging effect.'

'I suppose if he was very extravagant, it's possible.'

'Maybe.'

'What will you do tomorrow?'

'I'll have to go up to the Residence and talk to Archie again. I don't expect he'll relish raking over old events, but I want to know more about these rumours that Donald Moncrieff was seeing a woman and had run off with her. Where did they start and who spread them?'

'That might not be easy, dear. The nature of rumours is that they tend to be slippery when you try to pin them down.'

He sighed. 'I know, but potentially Marina Moncrieff is facing a very serious charge. It's no time to deal in assumptions, and if she turns out to be innocent, discovering who spread the rumours might provide me with alternative leads.'

Billy and Bella emerged from the shrubbery and trotted over to meet them as they got out of the car. De Silva bent down to stroke them. 'I think I'll leave Archie in peace for today,' he said, straightening up. 'But I'd better telephone Inspector Singh at Hatton and the Kandy station. I'd like them to be on notice as soon as possible that we're looking for Marina Moncrieff. She may even have got as far as Colombo by now if she drove through the night, so I'll call there too.'

They went into the drawing room and de Silva showed her the photograph of Marina and her husband.

'What a handsome couple they make,' observed Jane. 'She's very stylish, and that looks like a very expensive car.'

'A Bugatti. Apparently, it's the one he raced in, and it's vanished along with him. The photo must have been taken at least eight years ago, of course. Archie reckoned that Marina would be in her mid-thirties by now. Donald was, or is, fifteen or twenty years older than her. I'm afraid the photograph won't be a great help. It's pity that the sunglasses hide her eyes, but it's all I could find. I'll use it to get some missing person notices made and have them circulated but that will have to wait for the morning.'

* * *

The afternoon was well advanced by the time he had finished making his calls. He had caught up with Singh at home but had to contact the other stations direct. Being a Sunday, it had not been so easy to find the right people to issue instructions to mount a search for Marina Moncrieff.

'Sit down and have a rest, dear,' said Jane sympathetically when he came out to the verandah. 'Shall I have some tea brought out?'

'Thank you, but I think a walk around the garden will do me more good.'

He went down the steps and headed for the vegetable garden, Bella following in his wake. On the way he stopped in the shade of a lime tree and paused to smell the citrusy tang of its fruits, nestling like little green grenades amongst the leaves. Further on, he nipped off a few leaves of the mint growing in his herb patch. Rolling them between a finger and thumb, he sniffed them, thinking fondly of the deliciously fresh sambol they would make.

The powerful aroma of peppermint cleared his head. First thing tomorrow, he would get the printers to make the missing person notices and have them put up around Nuala and other places Marina might have reached. Then he would give Prasanna and Nadar the job of searching the area where the skeleton had been found. The chances of finding anything after eight years were slight, but he must close off that avenue. Whilst they were busy with that, he would pay a visit to Isobel Moncrieff. He wanted to know more about why she was so sure that her stepson had run off with this mistress of his.

He moved on to potter in the greenhouse; he always found it restful to tend to the plants that he and his gardener grew there. Bella leapt up on the staging and daintily picked her way between flowerpots and seed trays to an empty space that had been warmed by the sun. She lay down and stretched, then proceeded to wash her paws. De Silva was just finishing pinching out the tips of some geranium cuttings when he noticed that the sky had turned pink, shot with streaks of gold. Soon it would be dusk. He finished his task and wiped the soil from his hands. Bella's head lifted and she yawned, showing sharp little white teeth against a rose-pink mouth. He scratched her behind one ear and her eyes narrowed in bliss.

'Time to go in, little one. I expect your supper will be ready. I wonder what there is for you this evening. Some tasty fish perhaps.'

Bella jumped down from the staging and darted off in the direction of the bungalow. De Silva smiled. It was amazing how she understood what you said to her, although Jane claimed it wasn't the words that she understood but the tone you spoke them in.

After dinner, he and Jane went to sit on the verandah.

'Poor Archie,' said Jane. 'I can't help feeling a little sorry for him. I know it looks as if he did the wrong thing, but at the time it must have been tempting to sweep an unpleasant business under the carpet. And if none of the family was pressing for an investigation, there wouldn't have been much incentive to start one.'

Time in the garden, and a good dinner that included his favourite pea and cashew curry, dahl fragrant with caramelised onions and spices, and fried jackfruit chips had put him in a mellower mood where Archie was concerned.

'I suppose it isn't so hard to understand. I'll forgive him as long as he doesn't try to obstruct me now.'

'I'm sure he won't, dear.'

She was probably right. Whatever one said about Archie – and there were times when he found his boss infuriating – he was on the whole a fair-minded man.

'Shall we have some music this evening?' he asked.

'That would be nice. It seems ages since we listened to the gramophone.'

'Is there something you'd like?'

She shook her head. 'I don't mind. You choose.'

In the drawing room, he went over to the gramophone and thumbed through their record collection. It had grown over the years and was now quite extensive although records were costly in Ceylon as they had to be imported from England or America. He wasn't in the mood for anything classical this evening, and dance music seemed too energetic. He settled on Cole Porter, removed the record from its sleeve and put it on the turntable. As he went back to the verandah, the languid opening bars of *Begin the Beguine* drifted through the balmy evening air.

CHAPTER 5

The following morning, after he had arranged for the posters to be printed and spoken to the undertakers, he went to the station and brought Prasanna and Nadar up to date with events, also explaining the background to Donald Moncrieff's disappearance. The two young men looked slightly bemused, as well they might. It was a lot to take in.

'Do you think this gentleman did not run away with his lady friend after all, sir?' asked Prasanna.

'That's about the size of it, but we need proof, not just a hunch. I want to go back to the Moncrieff plantation now. We'll lock up the station so the pair of you can come with me. Two people are better than one for the job I have in mind.'

The journey to the plantation passed without hindrance from broken-down carts or runaway chickens. When de Silva parked the Morris at the house, the servant, Muttu, must have heard the car for he hurried out to meet them.

'There has been no word from the memsahib, Inspector,' he said anxiously.

'It's alright, Muttu. We've not come to check up on you. I want my men to search the area where the bones were found, and I want to pay a visit to Mr Moncrieff's stepmother. Please telephone her to say that I am on my way and give me directions.'

Muttu explained the route then de Silva took Prasanna and Nadar to the site of the grave before returning for the Morris and setting off.

* * *

Isobel Moncrieff's home was a bungalow, but a rather large one. Its paintwork looked fresher and its woodwork better cared for than that at the main house. Someone cared about the garden too. The shrubberies to either side of the gravel sweep in front of the property were neatly clipped, and there was a central bed filled with roses with not a weed in sight.

He went to the front door and looked for a bell to ring but there wasn't one. Instead, there was a brass knocker in the shape of a lion's head, so he rapped sharply. A few moments passed before he heard the rattle of a chain being undone. The door opened. A servant who looked considerably older than Muttu and a great deal less obliging regarded de Silva with an impassive expression on his face.

'Is Mrs Moncrieff in?'

'She is at breakfast.'

Eleven o'clock seemed a late hour for breakfast but de Silva didn't comment.

'Please tell her that Inspector de Silva of the Nuala police would like to speak to her. I understand my visit has been notified, but if it is inconvenient, I will return later.'

The servant murmured something, then leaving de Silva on the doorstep, went back inside. Whilst he waited, de Silva contemplated his surroundings. The dark-green paint on the front door was immaculate, and the lion's head knocker gleamed. The windows along the front of the bungalow looked spotless, but it was impossible to see into the rooms beyond because blinds were pulled down in each one. When he finally managed to get inside, though, he doubted he would find a cobweb-festooned ruin as Pip had done in Charles Dicken's *Great Expectations*, a book he had recently read. Isobel Moncrieff was probably exacting, even if she was reclusive, and her servant just ill-tempered. From the way Archie had described her, he had probably caught that from his mistress.

Just as he was beginning to think that he was to be left on the doorstep all morning in revenge for having given such short notice of his visit, the impassive servant reappeared. 'The memsahib will see you now.'

De Silva stepped inside, and as his eyes became accustomed to the change in the light from the brightness of the morning sunshine, he saw that the hallway was not at all gloomy. The walls were decorated with a pretty wallpaper patterned with leaves and flowers in the Chinese style. A vase of fresh flowers stood on a small side table, also in the Chinese style, and on either side of it there were high-backed mahogany chairs with cane seats.

The servant paused by the door at the end of the hall and stood aside for de Silva to enter. He stepped in and froze; a few feet away from him there was a tiger. Its lips were drawn back in a snarl, and white fangs gleamed in its cavernous, scarlet maw. De Silva's feet seemed glued to the floor as, heart thumping, he waited for it to spring. Then the servant moved between them, and he realised that there was the hint of a smile on the man's face. A tiger-skin rug: no doubt it was a little joke at the expense of new visitors that he enjoyed. On a side table nearby there was a framed photograph of several men and one woman dressed for hunting. A tiger carcass lay at their feet, presumably the same tiger that was now a rug.

Sufficiently recovered to turn his attention to the rest of the room, de Silva saw that it was airy and elegantly furnished with a view over the rear garden. Unusually, there seemed to be no verandah, but perhaps there was one elsewhere.

'Come in, Inspector. Let me have a look at you.'

The haughty, disembodied voice came from the direction of a wing chair upholstered with red velvet. Isobel Moncrieff was obviously bent on getting the upper hand. Resolving to do his best to counter her efforts with calm composure, de Silva approached across the turquoise and rose Persian carpet.

'It's good of you to see me at such short notice, ma'am. I trust you didn't have to hurry your meal.'

'Not at all, although breakfast is, I'm sure you will agree, the most important of them all.' He thought he detected a hint of mockery in her smile. In her day, he thought, she must have been a beauty. Even now, her classic features and high cheekbones gave her a very striking appearance, although the thick makeup she wore didn't completely conceal the lines on her forehead and the crows' feet around her eyes. Her hair was a soft shade of dove grey, arranged in a chignon, and she wore a flowing caramel-coloured ensemble with a string of pearls and delicate pearl earrings.

'I receive very few visits and certainly none from the authorities.' She placed a barely perceptible stress on the last word. 'I hope you haven't come to give me unpleasant news.'

'I'm afraid I have, ma'am. I expect you're aware that the Hill Country Challenge took place on Saturday.'

'Of course. When he was living in Nuala, my stepson Donald competed in all the rallies. Cars were a passion with him. Unfortunately, a very expensive one.'

'The rally was won by Johnny Perera.'

She frowned. 'Perera, you say. The name is familiar.'

'His family lived here at the plantation before your late husband bought the estate.'

'Ah yes, I remember Dudley Perera. He went on to make a great deal of money in rubber.'

'Johnny is his son. After he had celebrated his victory, he had a sudden desire to revisit his childhood home, so he and his friends drove up here.'

Isobel raised an eyebrow. 'I suppose you're about to tell me he assumed he would be welcomed at a late hour, even though he hadn't been invited.'

'Something like that, ma'am, although I don't believe he meant any harm. It was merely the exuberance of the day.'

'Forgivable. Please, go on. I hope my daughter-in-law was not alarmed by the intrusion.'

'She wasn't at home and still isn't.'

'Strange.' Isobel frowned. 'Marina rarely goes out, certainly not in the evenings. Last time I saw her, she didn't mention she had any plans to do so.'

'I spoke with Muttu. He said she'd not told him that she was going out, and her car has gone. He has no idea when she'll be back.'

'Well, it's unusual, but I'm not Marina's keeper. She isn't obliged to account to me, and certainly not to her servants. Was there a particular reason why you wanted to see her?'

'Mr Perera brought his dog, a German Shepherd, with him, and it ran off. When they found it, it had unearthed a bone. At first, they thought it must belong to an animal but then one of their party, a doctor, took the view that it was human. Further investigation revealed a skeleton buried in a disused area behind some garages.'

'Good heavens. What are you suggesting?' asked Isobel sharply.

'It's too soon to be certain, but I believe it's possible that the remains are those of your stepson.'

* * *

'Poor Marina,' whispered Isobel, half to herself. Her long, slim fingers twisted her necklace. Suddenly, she didn't seem quite as formidable as she had at first meeting. She looked away for a few moments, her head bowed, then turned back to face him. 'How much do you know of the story of Marina's marriage to my stepson?'

'The assistant government agent, Mr Clutterbuck, told me that they parted company about eight years ago.'

Isobel laughed dryly. 'A tactful way of putting it. Donald ran off with another woman. It was the last we've seen or heard from him.'

'Forgive me for asking, ma'am, I'm sure the subject is a painful one, but on what evidence do you base that conclusion?'

'My stepson had many liaisons over the years. Some of them were common knowledge, a fact that I found extremely distasteful. In this case, he was overheard making plans to leave Nuala with a mistress.'

'Heard by whom?'

'My companion, Miss Collins.'

'I'd like to speak to her if I may.'

'That won't be possible. Rosamund Collins left my employment shortly after Donald went away. I'm afraid she wasn't suited to the job.'

'Do you know where she went?'

Isobel thought for a moment. 'A family who lived near Ella. If I remember rightly, their name was Pelham. I've no idea if she's still with them.'

At least Ella was a small place. It shouldn't be too hard to track the Pelhams down, and even if this companion had moved on, it would be a start.

'If you're right that it's Donald's body you've found,' Isobel went on, 'I'm afraid Marina is likely to be very distressed. She and Donald weren't always happy, but every time he strayed, she took him back. I doubt I would be as forgiving, but life is hard for a woman on her own. I can testify to that. And she was certainly very much in love with him at the start. She's a clever young woman, and when they met in London, she was studying to become a doctor, but he swept her off her feet and she gave it all up to follow him to Ceylon.'

Isobel rallied. 'You may be wrong, of course. Do you have proof that they are Donald's remains you've unearthed, or is all this conjecture?'

'Nothing conclusive, but the circumstances are suspicious. More importantly, the skeleton bears signs of an injury that may help us to identify it. The left leg was broken in two places while the deceased was still alive. Do you recall your stepson having an accident at any time?'

'Whatever his faults, Donald was a good driver, but there may have been an incident I'm not aware of. My first husband, Harold Dacre, was a senior official in the Justice Secretariat. We lived in Colombo and I wasn't acquainted with the Moncrieff family. After he died, I married Donald's father, Victor. That was in 1925 and we hadn't known each other for very long. When I met Donald and Marina, they were dividing their time between here and Colombo where Donald had business interests. I have no idea what those were, so I'm afraid I can't enlighten you. There were also his motor racing activities which frequently took up his time. When Victor died in the autumn of 1930, Donald inherited the plantation. He and Marina moved into the main house and I came here.'

A pleading note entered her voice. 'Surely, you don't believe Marina had anything to with this. She's a gentle creature. If it is Donald, someone else must have killed him.'

'Do you know if he had any enemies?'

'Do you mean any who hated him enough to murder him? I have no idea. All I can tell you is that he wasn't a popular man.' She paused. 'Have you spoken to Peter Flint?

He manages the plantation for Marina. He may be able to tell you where she is.'

'I've already spoken to Mr Flint. He has no idea where she is either.'

'I'm sure there will be a perfectly simple explanation,' said Isobel briskly. 'And if this is Donald's body you've found, I repeat, nothing will convince me that she had a hand in his murder.'

'Your loyalty is admirable, ma'am. But I must ask you to notify me straight away if you see her.'

Isobel nodded. 'Of course.'

She rang the small brass bell on the table at her elbow. The impassive servant appeared almost immediately. He had probably been listening to every word.

'Show the inspector out, Jamis.'

De Silva took his leave. As he was ushered to the door, he thought how inappropriate the fellow's name was. He was far from exemplifying the good cheer that it meant. On the way back to collect Prasanna and Nadar, he decided he'd heard nothing so far that definitively ruled out Marina Moncrieff. In fact quite the reverse. Could it be a mere coincidence that Marina had disappeared the very night that what might well be the bones of her husband were discovered? If it wasn't a coincidence, how did she become aware they had been discovered? Had she seen the Perera party searching for the German Shepherd when it was barking from behind the garages, and realised the game might well be up?

However, he mustn't overlook the possibility that one of the sources of the rumour that Donald Moncrieff had run off with his mistress might be covering up their own or someone else's crime. He needed to find Rosamund Collins. He also needed Archie to tell him the name of anyone else who had offered information at the time of Moncrieff's disappearance.

CHAPTER 6

At the site of the grave, Prasanna and Nadar had searched within a wide radius but found nothing of interest.

'I suppose there have been eight years of monsoon rains since the body was buried,' said de Silva.

'And a landslide, sir,' added Prasanna, pushing a lock of hair out of his eyes with a mud-streaked hand.

Nadar, who was puffing a little, looked at him hopefully. 'Shall we stop, sir?' he asked.

'You may as well.' De Silva looked at his watch. 'If you were going to unearth any great revelations, I think you would have done so by now.'

The young men followed him back to the house and, after checking with Muttu that Marina had still not returned, de Silva drove home to Nuala and dropped them at the station.

'May we take time for lunch now, sir?' asked Nadar.

'You may, but don't take long over it. I want you to get over to the printers and collect the missing person notices I've ordered. Keep enough to put up in the usual places here and send the rest down to the police stations at Hatton, Kandy, and Colombo. By the time you come back, I'll probably have gone up to the Residence to speak with Mr Clutterbuck. You may as well hold the fort here.'

It wouldn't be advisable to go to the Residence straight away. Archie never liked to be interrupted at mealtimes.

The young men thanked him and hurried away. Left alone, de Silva's thoughts turned to his own lunch. Jane wasn't expecting him back, so he decided to eat at the bazaar.

Most people would already have done their food shopping, but the lanes between the stalls were crowded with lunchtime trade. The shops around the perimeter of the bazaar were also busy. Brightly coloured signs giving the names of their proprietors and assuring customers of the excellent quality and variety of goods on offer caught the eye. Bicycle and rickshaw bells provided a tinkling accompaniment to the general bustle.

De Silva dived into the lanes and headed for the area where his favourite stall was situated. On the way, he passed stalls displaying mounds of limes, pineapples, rambutans, mangosteens, durian fruits, and pomegranates. The vegetable stalls were equally colourful with earthy-smelling carrots, sweet potatoes, cauliflowers, and cabbages displayed alongside tomatoes, chillies, white or Bombay onions, and eggplants. Their colours varied from deep, glossy purple, to purple speckled with white, or butter yellow. There were all kinds of gourds including the long, knobbly bitter gourd that looked like an ugly reptile. He remembered his mother making an excellent relish from it that she flavoured with chilli and lime juice. Jackfruit, snake beans, and winged beans that were delicious when curried were also for sale.

Amongst the bundles of herbs, he saw gotu kola. The low, creeping plant with pretty penny-shaped leaves grew well in a patch at the bottom of his garden that was always boggy after the rains. It was prized in Ayurvedic medicine for fortifying the immune system, promoting restful sleep, and improving the circulation. Applied as an ointment, it was also believed to help wounds and burns to heal faster. His mother used to claim it was a good beauty treatment too, softening the skin and smoothing out wrinkles. Long ago, people had also noticed that elephants liked to munch the leaves, which had led to the belief that it would improve longevity and memory and even increase the power of thinking. He might need to resort to some of it before this case was over.

He reached the stall he was looking for and bought some kottu roti. A fresh batch was just being made, and he watched the stallholder take the balls of oiled dough and slap them on the metal counter at the back of the stall before cooking them on his sizzling hot griddle. Once they were cooked, he rolled them and deftly cut the rolls into slices then chopped those into small pieces. Vegetables, thinly sliced chillies, and a dollop of chicken curry were added and briskly mixed together. By the time the batch was ready, de Silva was even hungrier than he had been when he arrived at the bazaar. When he had finished the portion the stallholder gave him, he bought another.

He had almost finished it and was debating whether it was time to stop when he heard his name being called. He turned to see Charlie Frobisher and Ruth Bailey smiling at him. He greeted them, hoping there were no stray curls of vegetable clinging to his cheeks. A disadvantage of lunching in the street was that it could lead to undignified results.

'That looks good,' said Ruth. 'We ate here too. Charlie says it's one of the best places in town.'

'I agree with him there.'

'We're off to Colombo to stay with my uncle and aunt tomorrow. We thought we'd have a last look around the bazaar before we go. I was hoping to find a few presents to take with us.'

'I hope you were successful.'

'Yes, we've bought a lovely scarf for my aunt and two carved elephants that are very unusual for my uncle. He's very interested in woodwork.'

'Like my constable,' said de Silva with a smile. 'He is fond of carving toys for his children.'

'How's the Moncrieff case going?' asked Charlie.

De Silva raised an eyebrow. 'News travels fast.'

'I went up to the Residence this morning to have a word with the boss. He mentioned it then. It sounds a tricky one.'

'I'm afraid so. The trail will have gone very cold after so many years.' He didn't like to mention that Marina Moncrieff was his chief suspect. If he turned out to be wrong, it would be unfair to have blackened her name. Strictly speaking too, Charlie wasn't officially involved in the case, so he ought to be careful how much he told him.

Charlie lowered his voice. 'Between ourselves, I think the boss feels a bit guilty he didn't carry out a more thorough investigation at the time. He didn't say it in so many words, but you know the look he has when he's afraid he might be on sticky ground.'

De Silva knew it: the look of a mournful but recalcitrant bloodhound. He laughed. 'I do. Thank you for telling me.'

* * *

After his meeting with Charlie and Ruth, he headed back to the station. As he drove, he pondered over what he might have overlooked. David Hebden hadn't had long to investigate Doctor Lucas's notes, but the result of that was important. He needed proof that the dead man they were dealing with was indisputably Donald Moncrieff.

Then the thought of Perera's doctor, Michael Rudd, came into his mind. On reflection, he realised that he hadn't ascertained how thorough Rudd's examination of the remains had been. Given the situation and the fact that he'd appeared to be in a hurry to leave, it would be unwise to rely on it. That was something else he would need to enlist David Hebden's help with. Hopefully, he would be able to provide a theory as to the cause of death.

He was passing the front of the Crown Hotel when he noticed Rudd coming down the steps. He saw de Silva and raised a hand in greeting. Pulling the Morris into the shade of a nearby tree, de Silva got out and went over to speak to him.

'Good afternoon to you, Inspector. How are you getting on with ferreting out your Algie's identity?'

'Algie?'

Rudd smiled. 'The skeleton. At med school, we students called the one we were taught anatomy on "Algernon" – "Algie" for short.'

'Ah, I see. Nothing definite yet, but I'm glad we met. I've been wanting to ask if on reflection you noticed anything about the remains that might help to establish the cause of death.'

Rudd's brow furrowed. 'No, but I have to admit that the situation didn't encourage an exhaustive examination.'

'I appreciate that. I just wanted to check.'

A posse of servants emerged from the hotel carrying a large collection of monogrammed luggage. At the edge of the group, another servant was struggling to keep an excitable Caesar under control.

'As you see, we're on our way,' said Rudd. 'Mr Perera is due back in Colombo tomorrow.'

The man himself appeared at the top of the steps, dressed in an impeccably tailored cream linen suit and elegant tan leather shoes. His thick raven hair was slicked back in the latest fashion. He took the steps two at a time and joined them, holding out his hand to shake de Silva's.

'Good afternoon! I'm afraid we've caused you a bit of trouble with our little excursion. Rudd told me about it, and I learnt more when I lunched today with the Clutterbucks at the Residence. One doesn't like to speak ill of the dead, but if those bones are Donald Moncrieff's, I doubt he'll be much missed.'

'It hasn't been conclusively established that it is him yet.'

Perera smiled. 'So Clutterbuck said. But I had the impression he wasn't in much doubt.'

Interesting. Archie must have resigned himself to accepting that he had made a mistake in not investigating more thoroughly.

Caesar dragged his handler closer to his master's side and made a lunge to get the last bit of the way to him. De Silva wondered if the dog had accompanied the party to the Residence. A confrontation between Caesar and Angel would have been memorable.

'Mind what you're doing,' snapped Perera, glowering at the handler. The man hauled the big dog away, apologising abjectly. For a moment, de Silva saw a different side to his master and remembered Archie's story about how angry Perera had been when Donald Moncrieff had insulted him. He realised that he had never considered him as a suspect, and perhaps that had been an omission. But then if he had been involved, why return to the plantation now? The argument had been over Moncrieff's Bugatti. If Perera had a hand in his death, his best opportunity to take it would have been at the time.

But what if for some reason he had missed that opportunity? He had taken a considerable risk of being found at the property on Saturday night, but might he have known that Marina wouldn't be there? That would have made a difference. In some as yet mysterious way, was the Bugatti part of a connection between the dashing Perera and the unhappy Marina? Just how well had Perera known the Moncrieffs?

'In my early years in racing, Moncrieff was a regular fixture on the circuit, both here and in India,' he said when de Silva asked the latter question. 'Since the 1932 rally though, I've not come across either of the Moncrieffs anywhere. He was an abrasive fellow, not popular with other competitors, so he wasn't missed. It was put about that he was running through money at a great rate. I think that if people thought about him at all, it was to assume that he'd run out of funds. There was even talk that he'd gone abroad to join a team as a driver.'

'In your opinion, would that be likely?'

Perera shrugged. 'It's possible, although it would involve a loss of face. The sport's not exclusively the preserve of owners. There are some who like to own cars but prefer someone else to take the risks.' He smiled. 'My own father was eventually persuaded to accept his limitations, although he's never lost his taste for the excitement, even if it has to be obtained vicariously.'

'Thank you, sir. That's very helpful.' De Silva eyed the German Shepherd whose handler looked to be once again on the point of losing the battle. 'I wish you a safe journey,' he said quickly and returned to the Morris to continue on his way.

So, he thought to himself, if Perera had, contrary to what he said, come across either Moncrieff or Marina in the last eight years, there would need to be strong evidence to prove it.

* * *

It was almost three o'clock. Archie's siesta time should be over by now. He telephoned the Residence and waited while the servant who answered went to see if the assistant government agent was free to see him.

Half an hour later, he parked the Morris in a patch of shade on the Residence's drive. As the doorman let him into the entrance hall Florence Clutterbuck was coming down the stairs, her little household mop of a dog, Angel, tucked under one arm.

'Good afternoon,' she trilled. 'It's time for Angel's afternoon walk, but I don't know where the servant who usually takes him has got to. I rang the bell—' She stopped, and a frosty expression came over her face. 'Ah, there you are.'

A servant came hurrying into the hall carrying a small red lead. Florence's eyes fixed on his uniform tunic. 'Buttons,' she said sharply. The man fumbled to do up the top one, apologising hastily.

De Silva felt sorry for him. It was a very hot afternoon and he had probably been snatching a surreptitious nap.

Florence sniffed and put Angel down. 'I trust I won't need to remind you again.'

Angel trotted over to the servant and sat at his feet. He bent down and clipped on the lead. As he set off with the little dog trotting at his heels, de Silva was sure he heard him mutter something under his breath. He thought of the protests in India that were often in the news. These days, obedience to the British was not as unquestioning as it had been when he was a young man.

'I won't keep you,' said Florence as the Residence's imposing front door closed behind the pair. 'I expect you've come to see Archibald.'

It always amused de Silva that Florence persisted in using his boss's full name. It was rather a mouthful. He nodded and Florence came closer. 'What an unfortunate business this Moncrieff affair is,' she said sotto voce. 'Poor Archibald has been very put out. I do hope it will be handled discreetly.' She gave de Silva a meaningful look.

'That is my hope too, ma'am.'

'I'm pleased to hear it.'

She glanced around, presumably to satisfy herself they were still alone. 'Between ourselves, when Donald Moncrieff was in Nuala, there were rumours that he was violent towards his wife.'

'Are you aware of the source of these rumours, ma'am?'

Florence shook her head. 'You know how people talk, especially in a small town.'

De Silva knew very well. 'I understand that Marina Moncrieff wasn't very sociable, but did anyone try to befriend her?'

'It was difficult. She showed little or no interest in joining our local activities. Her husband's stepmother was much the same.' Florence frowned, perhaps remembering the incident of the spilt drink and the chastened official. 'I'm afraid I gave up after a while. I think most people did the same.'

So, in addition to whatever she had suffered at her husband's hands, Marina Moncrieff's life must have been a lonely one. Perhaps that was often the case where a woman was trying to hide a bad marriage, whether it was out of fear or shame. He wondered to what extent she had been able to confide in Isobel Moncrieff. From his brief meeting with her, he'd received the impression they were friendly but not very close. It was clear that Isobel had no time for her stepson, but she seemed to be a strong character who would not let anyone undermine her. If Marina had been less sure of herself, might she have become desperate enough to choose murder as a way out?

A servant entered the hall and came over to them. 'There is a telephone call for you, memsahib. Mrs Peters asks if you have time to speak with her.'

'Ah, the vicar's wife. I expect it will be about the new rota for the church flowers. I'll come.' She bestowed a gracious smile on de Silva. 'Goodbye, Inspector. I'm glad we had the opportunity for our little chat.'

* * *

Not needing to be shown the way, de Silva headed off in the direction of Archie's study. As he walked along the familiar corridor lined with hunting prints, he wondered how much Archie had told Florence and how much she had divined from his behaviour. Wives had a way of reading one's mind.

He knocked on the study door and heard his boss call out for him to come in. When he did so, Darcy hauled himself up from his place beside Archie's chair and ambled over to greet him. De Silva rubbed him behind the ears, and after a few moments, the elderly Labrador returned to Archie's side and flopped down again with a grunt. The room gave off its usual aroma of tobacco and dog and was as untidy as ever. Was Archie going to tell him that he'd been unable to find anything about the Moncrieff case? He was mildly reassured when his boss pointed to a slim file.

'Sit yourself down. All the information's in there. You can take it away with you if you wish, but I suggest you take a look now in case you have any questions.'

'Thank you, sir.'

It wasn't a long read. Archie had located his papers concerning Donald Moncrieff's disappearance and he had interviewed Isobel Moncrieff's companion, Rosamund Collins, at the time. The information she had given back then matched what Isobel had told de Silva that morning. Archie didn't appear to have asked searching questions though, and plenty came to mind. Had Rosamund Collins overheard Donald talking to his lover on more than one occasion? Was she able to give dates and approximate times? What had made her so sure it was a lover? Had she heard him use any endearments that indicated it was the case? Did she catch a name? From his manner, did she have the impression he was wary of being overheard? The notes didn't answer any of these questions. It also occurred to de Silva that if Donald made the call or calls from his own home, as presumably he did, what was Rosamund Collins doing up there?

'I must have asked that kind of thing at the time,' said Archie when de Silva, trying to be as tactful as possible, raised some of the points. He frowned. 'I believe it was only one occasion. And as to why she was there, there was something about returning a book for Isobel Moncrieff.'

It wasn't a very compelling explanation. The possibility crossed de Silva's mind that the companion had jumped to conclusions. Or was there a more sinister reason? Clearly, she hadn't been a favourite with Isobel, but had she known something of Marina's plight and felt sorry for her? Did she think that the circumstances in which Donald disappeared were suspicious? In short, with or without Marina's knowledge, had she lied to protect her? The need to find Rosamund Collins had just increased.

'Did you also speak with Isobel Moncrieff at the time, sir?'

'Naturally, but it was a dashed awkward business. None of us likes scandal attaching to our family name, but she made her distaste abundantly clear.'

De Silva was sure that she had done. It can't have been hard for a woman like Isobel to make use of Archie's gentlemanly instincts to put him off. De Silva had observed that, with the possible exception of when they were in private with their closest relations – where he was in no position to vouch for it – the British men he had come across had difficulty dealing with the opposite sex on anything apart from a social level. It was no surprise that Archie had not taken any notes.

'What about Marina Moncrieff?' The file also contained very little about Archie's interview with her. Again, the awkwardness of the British male in the face of strong emotions probably played a part in that.

'She was understandably upset. I didn't like to add to her distress with a lot of questions.'

The suspicion might turn out to be unfair, but had Marina manipulated Archie?

De Silva looked back at the file. 'I see that a gentleman called Colonel McTaggart approached you.'

Archie reached for the box on his desk, took out a cigarette and lit it. De Silva smelt a whiff of sulphur as he shook out the match. 'Yes. I was rather surprised when he turned up and said he'd heard Moncrieff was missing. He was particularly keen to know what was being done to find him and to be kept in the picture.'

'Did he give a reason for that?'

'Something about Moncrieff owing him money. He seemed very put out about it. Understandable I suppose, but His Majesty's government isn't in the business of collecting private debts. I told him he'd be notified as a matter of courtesy if Moncrieff turned up, but that was all.'

'Did anyone else come forward?'

'Not that I recall.'

'How did Colonel McTaggart hear that Donald Moncrieff had gone missing?'

From the attitude of Moncrieff's nearest and not very dearest, de Silva would have been surprised if they had reported his disappearance. Given the remoteness of the plantation, would there be neighbours to wonder why they hadn't seen him for a while? Perhaps business contacts had queried his absence.

'As I am now, I was then president of the Nuala branch of the Royal Automobile Association,' said Archie. 'Moncrieff was a committee member at the time, so when I became aware that he wasn't attending meetings or answering letters, I told one of my staff to make enquiries, but he drew a blank. Perhaps there was something similar on McTaggart's part, but I have no clear recollection.'

He stubbed out his cigarette. 'But we still don't have conclusive proof that these remains are Moncrieff's. Unless something's happened since yesterday that you're not telling me.'

'There's nothing, sir. I spoke with Doctor Hebden, and he doesn't remember Moncrieff having an accident, but he promised to look through his predecessor's notes in case there was a record of one before he came to Nuala.'

'Ah yes, Doctor Lucas. Good chap – one of the old school. Always maintained there weren't many things that fresh air and brisk exercise wouldn't put right.'

De Silva could understand how that attitude would appeal to Archie. He hoped Doctor Lucas wasn't an advocate of cold baths as well.

'Has Hebden come back to you yet?' asked Archie.

'Not yet.'

'I assume you asked Isobel Moncrieff if she recalled her stepson having an accident.'

'She told me she wasn't aware of one.'

'It strikes me Marina Moncrieff would be wise to sell the plantation and move on. If it turns out that these bones aren't her husband's, she could find a lawyer to investigate the presumption of death business on her behalf and try to resolve matters that way. She must still be a relatively young woman and a good-looking one as I recall. Even if the place hasn't done well in the last few years, there's a lot of land there. I expect it would easily fetch enough for her to set herself up in a smaller place. Maybe move to Kandy or even Colombo. She might marry again, but she certainly won't find another husband if she carries on mouldering away in the middle of nowhere.'

'At this stage, I don't think we can rule out the possibility that she was involved, sir, and of course, the law cannot be used to allow a criminal to profit from his or her crime.'

Archie looked irritable. 'Naturally.'

He stood up. 'Well, if there's nothing more I can help you with, I think I'll finish up here and take this fellow for his walk now it's cooler.'

Darcy opened his eyes and scrambled to his feet.

'I'd like to speak with Colonel McTaggart, sir. Do you know where he's to be found?'

'I expect one of the secretaries can give you the address.'

* * *

Back at the Morris, de Silva realised that he'd spent longer than he'd anticipated with Archie. Shadows stretched over the Residence's manicured lawns and flowerbeds, and the sun was dipping towards the horizon. In the cooling air, a nearby bed of lilies gave off an intense fragrance. A vivid-green flock of parrots swooped down to roost in one of the trees, squabbling as they jostled for position.

Before going home, he stopped off at the station. Prasanna and Nadar had dealt with the posters and were in the public room, talking with a man who had come to report that his neighbour's goats had trespassed on his vegetable patch and eaten their way through his crops. The neighbour had already removed the goats but was refusing to repair the fence on the grounds that he had no money to do so. De Silva was pleased to see that his officers, particularly Prasanna, seemed to be doing a good job of taking charge of the situation. They had already promised that the neighbour would receive a visit in the morning and be ordered to do the work. If he had no money, he could find fallen wood in the jungle or sell one of his own goats and buy it. Reasonably mollified, the man left.

De Silva filled them in on the information he'd received from Archie. 'When you've dealt with these troublesome goats,' he finished, 'I want one of you to contact the post office in Ella. It should be possible to telephone there. I want to trace this lady, Rosamund Collins. She was last heard of working for a family called Pelham. Find out where they live and get me the details. If we're lucky, she'll still be with them, but if not, they should know the address she went on to.'

'Do you want us to contact them straight away, sir?' asked Prasanna.

'Just their address will be enough for the moment. After that, if there's nothing urgent on your desks, you may go home.'

* * *

By the time he reached Sunnybank it was dark. Jane was in the drawing room sorting through a box of oddments. She offered her cheek for him to kiss.

'What are you up to there?' he asked.

'Oh, only picking out a few things to donate to the jumble sale Florence is planning. She's raising money for one of her good causes.'

De Silva had to admit that although Florence was bossy, her charitable activities had to be admired.

'I saw her this afternoon when I went up to the Residence to speak to Archie. She collar-held me in the hall as I went in.'

'It's collared or buttonholed, dear.'

'Hmm.'

'About this Moncrieff business, I suppose.'

'Naturally.'

Jane held up a skein of pale pink wool. 'I think there's enough here to make something small for the jumble sale. A baby's cardigan perhaps.' She rolled it into a ball and added it to the wool already in the bag at her feet. 'There, I think that's enough wool. I'm sure I can find some books we're not likely to reread. What did Florence have to say about the case?'

'She wanted me to be aware that Archie's troubled by it, and it needs to be handled discreetly.'

Jane snorted. 'As if you'd do anything else, but then one can't blame her for being loyal to him.'

'I suppose not.' He looked around. 'Where have Billy and Bella got to?'

'They went to the kitchen for their tea. Cook is a little late with it today. I expect they'll be back soon.'

He had to admit to feeling rather put out. Since the cats had arrived in their lives, he had grown accustomed to a welcoming committee. As if on cue, Bella trotted in and weaved herself around his legs, purring. He bent down to pick her up. There were a few tiny flecks of milk on her whiskers, and a faint smell of fish rose to his nostrils. A moment later Billy arrived too.

'So, tell me what else happened today,' said Jane.

He described his visit to Isobel Moncrieff's house and his impression that she had been glad to see the back of her stepson.

'How sad it is when families don't get on,' said Jane. 'But it might have been hard for Donald to accept a new woman in his father's life. Particularly if he was very fond of his mother. I forget who told me, but I believe she died when he was quite young.'

'If a name comes back to you, let me know. It might be important. I'd like to interview anyone who was close to the family. Although I'd be surprised if there are many of those about,' he added.

'What did she have to say about Marina's disappearance?'

'She refused to believe Marina killed Donald. Interestingly, she told me she thought Marina still cared for him despite his infidelity. Apparently, she was training to be a doctor when they met, and she gave it all up to marry him and come out to Ceylon.'

'It sounds very romantic. How sad it ended so badly.'

'Yes, though it's possible things may have got even more complicated since.' He had been thinking more about how Perera might be involved in the crime.

'What do you mean?'

'Perera took a considerable risk that he would be found by Marina at the plantation on Saturday night. He might have had difficulty explaining to her what he was doing there. On reflection, the business about wanting to revisit his old home and hoping to see at least one of Moncrieff's collection of cars sounds rather lame to me. Who does that kind of thing in the middle of the night, especially uninvited? But what if Marina wasn't there in the first place and Perera knew she wouldn't be? There would be no risk of an awkward encounter with her.'

'So, are you suggesting that he and Marina might have been in contact shortly before the race? Could they have been romantically involved at some time? Perhaps he killed Donald Moncrieff at her bidding, but later she broke off the affair. He wanted to rekindle it and was rejected.' She frowned. 'Didn't Archie say something about Perera making Donald Moncrieff an offer for his Bugatti and Moncrieff refusing him very rudely? As it's such an expensive car, maybe Perera had the idea that if he could find it, he'd take it in revenge for being rejected.'

De Silva laughed. 'No, my love, this isn't a plot from one of your detective novels. My idea is this. What if Moncrieff owed Perera money and never repaid it before he disappeared? Perera assumed he'd never see Moncrieff again and sought the cash from Marina. Marina might reasonably have pleaded poverty so Perera might have wanted to verify that. He told her he would be in Nuala and would visit her on the evening of the race. She was suspicious and told him not to bother as she would be away. She then booked herself into a hotel somewhere, simply to avoid him.'

He paused and rubbed his chin. 'Now, what if Perera came up with the idea that in view of Marina's lack of co-operation, he would take the Bugatti in lieu of repayment? Possibly he lied to his friends about the visit to the plantation being a purely nostalgic one, or he may have intended to go alone, but fuelled by the party atmosphere, his friends insisted on being with him as a bit of an adventure. What then if he found that the Bugatti was no longer at the plantation? The discovery of the skeleton intervened and Perera concluded Marina must have done away with Moncrieff. He decided Marina was too dangerous to cross over a debt that had been outstanding for many years and he was best to forget it.'

He glanced at Jane who was laughing. 'I see you're not convinced.'

'And you accuse me of borrowing theories from detective novels! In any case, mine is far more exciting.'

'Mine may not be as exciting, my love, but some of it may be true. I'd need clear proof, of course, before taking on someone like Perera, but I can't rule out him at least withholding evidence.' He sighed. 'Or maybe your theory is the right one, and Perera is our murderer. On the other hand, maybe I'm just tired…'

Jane looked at him affectionately. 'No, dear, you are right to look at all options. What about Archie? Did he have anything helpful to tell you?'

'There wasn't much in the notes he made at the time. Apart from Isobel and Marina, neither of whom he appeared to question closely, he spoke with Isobel's companion, a lady called Rosamund Collins, and a man named McTaggart who had business dealings with Donald.' He recounted what they had both told Archie.

'McTaggart?' Jane reached to stroke Billy who had jumped on the back of the sofa and padded along it to nuzzle her ear. 'His wife often comes to church events, but on her own. She's a pleasant enough lady but a terrible gossip. I wonder how he knew Donald was missing. And if Archie was doing his best to keep that quiet, why did McTaggart go to him for information?'

'Archie was rather vague about that, but he said McTaggart was trying to recover some money Donald owed him.' He yawned. 'I'll go and change out of my uniform, then shall we have a drink before dinner?'

'That would be lovely.'

When he returned, comfortable in loose white trousers and tunic, she had put away the box of oddments and the bag for Florence. De Silva poured their drinks, and they took them out to the verandah. It was a clear night, and the sky was full of stars.

'I saw Charlie Frobisher and his friend Ruth at the bazaar this afternoon,' he said when they had talked a little more about the case. 'They're off to Colombo tomorrow.'

'I liked her very much. I'm so glad Charlie's found such a nice girl. I do hope they stay together.'

De Silva smiled. 'I agree they seem very well suited.'

But, he reflected, these were uncertain times. They might not have a choice. With a war on, either of them could be posted elsewhere at any time. Still, it didn't do to spoil a beautiful evening dwelling on things one could do nothing about. It was enough for him trying to keep law and order in Nuala.

The clock in the drawing room struck eight. 'Dinner should be ready soon,' said Jane.

'Good, I'm hungry. I only had a snack in the bazaar at lunchtime.'

After dinner, they settled down in the drawing room to read. De Silva had decided not to tackle another of Dickens' novels just yet. He picked up the poetry anthology Jane had given him for Christmas. He had enjoyed the ones he'd read so far. He remembered learning some of them at school, but it had seemed rather a chore then. Perhaps poetry was something to be savoured later in life. He embarked on Shelley's *Ozymandias*.

CHAPTER 7

The day had only just dawned, but although de Silva had passed a restless night, he didn't want to go back to sleep. Stealthily, so as not to wake Jane, he climbed out of bed, put on his dressing gown and slippers, and crept out of the room. As he opened the door to the verandah, the drop in temperature outside made him shiver. Tendrils of mist curled around the trees and shrubs. Billy and Bella, who had joined him, slipped past into this ghostly world and melted into the milky air.

Leaving the verandah door ajar for them, he turned back into the drawing room and sat down in his favourite chair. The problem of identifying the human remains had preoccupied him in his wakeful hours. What if David Hebden didn't come up with anything? Even though it wouldn't be easy to explain how anyone other than Donald Moncrieff had been buried in that patch of wilderness, if he was to hold Archie to his promise to reopen the case, he would need to convince him Donald was dead.

Then there was Marina. Hopefully, one of the police stations whose help he had requested would have information for him today as to her whereabouts. He had stressed that the matter was urgent, but all the same, it might be worth making a few calls to keep his colleagues on their toes.

Bella sidled through the door from the verandah and came to jump on his lap; her fur smelled of damp grass.

She regarded him with her jade-green eyes and miaowed. How pleasant to have nothing to think about except for how soon the next meal would arrive.

He returned to the problem in hand. The other job he must do today was pay a visit to Colonel McTaggart. He would call Archie's secretary and ask for the address. Had Moncrieff owed him a lot of money? Most men had their pride and didn't like to be made fools of, so it might be a delicate question. He'd have to approach it with care.

'Ah, there you are. I was worried. Are you alright?' Jane had come into the room.

He rolled his shoulders, easing the stiffness in them. 'Yes, but I woke early and couldn't get back to sleep. I didn't want to disturb you.'

'I suppose you were thinking about the case.'

He nodded. 'I'll visit this man Colonel McTaggart later. I'm hoping he'll be able to tell me something about Moncrieff's business interests. Isobel said he was generally unpopular, but she may not have been aware of whether he made any enemies in business.' He sighed. 'As for the rest, tracking down Marina Moncrieff is beginning to seem like finding a needle in a haystack. I suppose we should check local hotels and hospitals just in case, but this needs a far larger number of men than I have.'

He rubbed his eyes. 'Perhaps breakfast will buck me up.'

* * *

After breakfast he telephoned the Residence for the address then set off to find the McTaggarts' house. He noted it was in an area where the less affluent members of the British community lived.

The bungalow stood by itself at the end of a narrow track. It was small and rather drab looking, but it appeared to be surrounded by a fair amount of land, a considerable proportion of it still virgin jungle. De Silva noticed that the short drive leading up to it hadn't received any attention for a long time. The gravel surface had worn thin and weeds encroached from the overgrown borders on either side. He parked the Morris then went to the front door and rang the bell. Eventually, a servant arrived.

'Is Colonel McTaggart at home? My name is Inspector de Silva and I'd like to speak with him.'

Before the servant had time to answer, de Silva heard the sound of a woman's voice drifting from within. 'Who is it, Gunadasa?'

The servant made a little bow. 'Please wait a moment, sahib.' He turned back into the hall and a short conversation ensued before a tiny, birdlike lady appeared.

'Good morning, Inspector. I'm Mrs McTaggart. How can I help you?'

'If it's not inconvenient, ma'am, I'd like a word with your husband.'

Mrs McTaggart looked puzzled. 'May I ask why?'

'I hope he will be able to help with an inquiry I'm engaged on.'

'Nothing serious, I hope.'

'I think it will be more straightforward if I explain to him in person. Is he at home?'

A slight show of reluctance on her face, Mrs McTaggart stepped back to let him enter. 'He's in the garden. I'll take you there.'

She led him along a narrow hallway that, like the drive, looked as if it hadn't been given any attention for many years. The paintwork was scuffed and apart from a few framed prints depicting ruined castles and lakes surrounded by brooding pines, there was no furniture except for a small table and a hat stand both made of darkly varnished wood. The drawing room Mrs McTaggart led de Silva into was equally dispiriting. As they emerged onto the verandah, a loud crack rent the air. Recognising gunshot, de Silva tensed and froze, but although she winced, he was surprised to see that Mrs McTaggart showed no sign of alarm.

'My husband likes to practise his aim in the mornings. Fortunately, we have no close neighbours.'

Another report was followed by a tirade of angry noises. De Silva became increasingly apprehensive then jumped back as a small troop of langur monkeys raced into sight. Their eyes bulged and they were chattering furiously. Not slowing pace, they hurtled into a nearby grove of trees and swarmed up to shelter in the branches.

'Hamish!' Mrs McTaggart paused then called out again, this time louder.

'What is it, woman?' The voice had a strong accent that de Silva recognised as Scottish. Its owner rounded the corner from another part of the garden, red-faced and scowling, a shotgun in the crook of his arm. De Silva was relieved to see that he carried it with the action open. If shooting was one of his regular activities, it was no wonder his wife hadn't seemed to turn a hair.

'This is Inspector de Silva, Hamish. He would like to have a word with you about an inquiry he's pursuing.'

McTaggart's scowl deepened as he stared at de Silva. 'Can't think what it can be, but no doubt you'll enlighten me.' He gestured to the bungalow. 'I think we'll go to my study.'

In the study, a rattan chair with a faded paisley cushion on the seat creaked under de Silva's weight as he sat down. He waited while McTaggart carefully stowed the shotgun in a gun rack and placed a belt containing unused cartridges on the shelf below the racking. The rack contained several more guns that, unlike the other contents of the house de Silva had seen, were polished and gleaming.

McTaggart sat down behind his desk. 'Now, what's this about?'

'I believe you were acquainted with Donald Moncrieff.'

The Scotsman's gruff expression turned thunderous. 'As ill luck would have it, I was. But he's been gone from Nuala for years. Ran off with some woman, I was told. Not been heard of since. Why do you ask about him now?'

'A skeleton has been found buried in an unfrequented area of the plantation where he lived. There's a possibility that it's his.'

McTaggart frowned. 'You mean you suspect he was murdered?'

De Silva nodded. 'I understand you went to Mr Clutterbuck shortly after Mr Moncrieff disappeared following the 1932 Hill Country Challenge and asked what efforts were being made to trace him. You were anxious to be informed of his whereabouts if he was found.'

'I was.' The scowl returned. 'Clutterbuck wasn't much help.'

'Why were you so keen to find Mr Moncrieff, sir?'

'He'd borrowed money off me and kept refusing to repay it.'

'May I ask what kind of sum was involved?'

McTaggart was silent for a few moments, then he glanced at the study door, stood up, and went over to close it before sitting down again. 'I suppose I may as well tell you the whole truth. Better you hear it from me. Donald Moncrieff persuaded me into an investment that turned out to be a swindle. To this day, I'm convinced he knew it was much riskier than he revealed but he needed backers. My parents had recently died, and I inherited what one might call "a substantial sum". I should never have let him talk me into it,' he added bitterly. 'It's not a mistake I'll make twice. To this day, I'm convinced that he made money, even if investors like myself didn't. My wife only knows the half of it. I told her I'd lent Moncrieff a small amount because he'd come to me saying he was temporarily in difficulty, and he hadn't repaid me. I'd be grateful if you would keep the true position to yourself.'

'Of course. Was there anyone else involved?'

'Several people. I can tell you their names if you wish.'

De Silva pulled out his notebook and jotted down the names McTaggart gave him.

'Do you happen to have addresses for any of these gentlemen?' he asked.

McTaggart opened the desk drawer to his right and pulled out a leather-bound book. 'I'll give you the ones I've got written down here. But since I retired, I've lost touch with a lot of people, and their addresses may have changed.'

When de Silva had finished writing down the addresses, he looked up to find that McTaggart was watching him warily. 'If they are Moncrieff's remains you've found, I hope you're not suggesting I had a hand in his death.'

'At the moment, I'm only trying to build up a picture of events around the time he disappeared.'

McTaggart grunted. 'All I can tell you is that I'd been pressing for information, in the hope I'd get back at least some of the money the wretched bounder persuaded me to invest.'

'Did you speak with anyone else who had invested?'

'A few, but it was awkward.'

That was understandable. Admitting to what had happened must have cost McTaggart himself a considerable amount in loss of pride.

'Incidentally, how did you find out that he was missing?'

'My wife heard it from Moncrieff's stepmother, Isobel.'

'Were they friendly?'

'They were at one time, but you'd better ask my wife about that.'

'Thank you, I will. How would you describe your relations with Mr Moncrieff?'

McTaggart let out a harsh bark of laughter. 'Before he

revealed his true colours, do you mean? I suppose I thought him a pleasant enough chap. He had an expensive lifestyle, but I assumed the profits from the plantation and whatever else he inherited from his father funded that. I found out the hard way that his finances were less straightforward. And after he disappeared, I learned through a variety of channels that he had plenty of enemies.'

'Can you give me any names?' asked de Silva, pencil poised over his notebook.

McTaggart shrugged. 'My fellow investors, of course.'

'May I ask where you were around the time of the 1932 rally?'

'Here in Nuala. My wife and I travelled a great deal during my days in the army. Since I retired, we've been happy to stay put.' He paused. 'If you've no more questions, I'll take you to see my wife.'

* * *

Mrs McTaggart was still in the garden speaking with one of her servants. Nearby, a target had been set up on the lawn. Presumably, it was the one McTaggart used to practise his shooting. De Silva was relieved to see there were no langur monkey corpses in evidence.

'Margaret!'

Mrs McTaggart looked up then hastily dismissed the servant.

'The inspector has a question for you,' said McTaggart, striding over to her. 'He's investigating a murder.'

Margaret McTaggart looked alarmed. 'Who has been murdered?'

'We're not sure yet, ma'am,' said de Silva calmly. 'But a skeleton has been found that may be that of Donald Moncrieff. Your husband tells me that back in 1932, after the Nuala car rally, you heard it from his stepmother Isobel that he had disappeared.'

'I did.' She looked anxious. 'She told me in confidence, but I didn't think it would do any harm to tell Hamish. Isobel was anxious to keep the matter quiet. She wanted to avoid a scandal, not just on her own account but also for Marina. Until she told me, I hadn't realised what a wretched marriage the poor girl had been forced to endure. Isobel said most of Donald's flings with other women hadn't lasted long, but this time she believed it was more serious. It would take Marina time to recover her self-respect, and she might never do so completely, but Isobel really believed it would be for the best if Donald stayed away for good.'

'Was Mrs Moncrieff in the habit of confiding in you?'

A look of sadness came over Margaret McTaggart's face. 'At one time I would have said so. I thought we were good friends. But after Donald disappeared, I began to notice a change. It happened quite slowly, but she withdrew into herself. Marina was the same. I wondered if they found it easier to cope with life that way. No one likes to be pitied, do they, Inspector? News eventually got around that Donald had left.' She flushed. 'I hope Isobel and Marina didn't think I had anything to do with it.'

De Silva didn't like to pursue the point. Jane had indicated that Mrs McTaggart was a gossip, but whether she had been the one to spread the story was not very important to know. The interesting piece of information was that Isobel Moncrieff had confided in her. If he were to be asked to name a lady who was unlikely to entrust her family's secrets to a friend, it would be Isobel Moncrieff. Had she chosen Margaret McTaggart precisely because she expected that the lady wouldn't be able to resist the temptation to divulge them to others? Was this proof that Isobel had been exerting herself to protect Marina?

CHAPTER 8

'Was the visit worthwhile?' asked Jane when he arrived home.

She shuddered when he came to the part about the shotgun. 'Those poor monkeys. I'm surprised they haven't decamped for good. I'm glad he didn't hurt any of them.'

'I noticed plenty of bullet holes in the target. He's probably a good shot.'

'That must be a relief to Margaret.' She paused before continuing. 'It's strange how one can be acquainted with someone for years and have so little knowledge of what their home life is like. Margaret's always well dressed and seems happy, but do you think they have money worries?'

'It's hard to say. Clearly McTaggart lost a significant amount of money in this investment. But I can only guess at the extent to which it has harmed their financial situation. The bungalow was shabby, but it doesn't necessarily prove they're hard up. Some people are not interested in that kind of thing. The garden was large and very pretty. Perhaps Mrs McTaggart takes more pleasure in that. Hopefully, for most of the time she's able to enjoy it without needing to dodge bullets. She may not be aware of any money problems. He indicated that he doesn't tell her everything.'

'I don't think I should like that,' said Jane.

He laughed. 'Then I must tell you about these gambling debts I've been running up.'

She picked up a cushion and threw it at him; he caught it deftly. 'Only joking.'

'Good. Now seriously, do you think we should be looking on the colonel as a suspect?'

'It's too early to rule anyone out completely, but he's not high on my list. Nor are any of the other investors McTaggart told me about, although I'll keep hold of their addresses for the moment. From where we found the skeleton, however, the most plausible explanation seems to be that the murder took place at the plantation. Otherwise, the killer would have had to transport the body all the way out there to bury it, and it would have been difficult to do that without being spotted.'

'And how would McTaggart or the other investors have known about the area where the grave was dug? I agree it's far more likely the murder was carried out by someone who knew the plantation well and could move about it without attracting suspicion.'

'So that narrows the field to the family or the staff, not forgetting Perera, of course. We're back to my needing to find Marina as soon as possible.'

'I see why you hang on to the possibility of Perera being involved but I also wonder if Peter Flint was telling the truth when he said he had no idea where Marina was. From what you told me about him and what I remember of her, they would also make an attractive couple. If he was running the plantation and her husband wasn't taking much interest, she might have become reliant on Flint. It would be easy for that to lead to something more, especially if she was lonely and wanted someone to comfort her.'

He turned the idea over in his mind and this time didn't make light of Jane's contribution. 'You may have something there. In any case, I've been thinking that another trip to the plantation might be helpful. Although Flint mentioned that the plantation still wasn't doing as well as it should, the land looked in good order to me. I might pay a visit to that office of his later on tonight and see what I can find out from the accounts. There may be ledgers that will show how the place is really doing. Maybe Flint has been deliberately recording low profits, either to keep some of them for himself, and if you're right, Marina, or in case Moncrieff came back and started squandering money again.'

'But the latter would mean Flint believed he might return,' said Jane.

'Yes, leading us back to the idea that if Marina is guilty, she acted on her own.'

'You will be careful, won't you? It's very remote up there if anything goes wrong. Why not take Prasanna or Nadar with you?'

'Maybe I'll take one of them. I'll think about it.'

'Just promise me you won't indulge in any foolish heroics.'

'Account ledgers are more likely to be dusty than dangerous.'

'As long as they're all you encounter.'

'Don't worry. I'll take care that no one is around before I go in. I noticed the plantation office when I went down with Flint to speak to the workers. It's a good distance from the main house and Isobel's bungalow.'

'What about where he lives?'

'I haven't been there, so I'm not sure, but I promise you I'll take care.'

Jane rested her chin on her hand. 'I still think it's odd that Isobel confided in Margaret McTaggart. I don't recall them being friends but then at the time Donald Moncrieff disappeared, we hadn't been in Nuala long, and I hadn't got to know anyone well. Florence might remember. I could ask her if you like.'

'Why not? But please make sure she understands she mustn't mention you've asked.'

'You needn't worry. Whatever her faults, she knows how to be discreet when it's important. I don't suppose there's been any news of Marina yet?'

'I didn't look in at the station on the way home, but I'll go straight after lunch. I hope Prasanna and Nadar will have tracked down this family that Rosamund Collins went to work for after she left Isobel. If they have, I may have to go up to Ella to see them unless I can reach them on the telephone.'

One of the servants appeared at the door to the verandah, announcing that lunch was ready. In his enjoyment of an excellent curry made of green beans, a dish of spiced cauliflower, a deliciously creamy dahl and several tasty side dishes, de Silva almost forgot that he still seemed to be a long way off from solving this case.

After they had finished the meal with slices of mango, papaya, and banana, he dipped his fingers in the bowl of water by his plate and wiped them on his napkin. 'Delicious.'

He stood up and came around to Jane's side of the table to kiss her cheek. 'I'm sorry to hurry away, but there may be a lot to do this afternoon.'

'Will you telephone me if you're going to be late?'

'Of course.'

Jane smiled. 'When have I heard that before?'

* * *

Prasanna was just putting down the telephone when de Silva came into the station. He and Nadar both looked pleased with themselves.

'I take it you've had a successful morning.'

'Yes, sir. The matter of the goats is all sorted out,' said Prasanna. He held out a piece of paper. 'And the postmaster in Ella confirms that the Pelham family still live there. He gave me their address and telephone number.'

'So, I may as well retire,' said de Silva.

Briefly, Prasanna looked chastened, but then he must have noticed the twinkle in his boss's eye for he smiled. 'Not yet I hope, sir.'

De Silva took the piece of paper. He was glad to hear that the Pelhams owned a telephone. The road from Nuala to Ella was rough and winding. The journey was more pleasantly accomplished by train, where one could enjoy the magnificent views of hills covered by tea plantations, but the train journey was a slow one, and he was keen to find Rosamund Collins as soon as possible.

His call was answered by a servant who went to fetch Mrs Pelham.

'Miss Collins left us almost four years ago,' she said when de Silva had explained what he wanted to know. She sounded puzzled. 'May I ask why you want to contact her?'

'We think she may have information relevant to an inquiry into events that happened in Nuala while she lived here. I hasten to say, there's no suggestion that she is implicated except as a witness.'

'I'm glad to hear it. I always found her a very respectable lady. It wasn't through our choice that she left.'

'What was the reason for her going?'

'She'd come to us to act as a companion to my mother who became very fond of her, but when my mother died, Rosamund decided that she wanted to enter a convent. We weren't surprised. She was a quiet, gentle person and her faith was clearly very important to her. We heard from her from time to time after she left us, and I had the impression that she had at last found the life that was right for her.'

De Silva reached for his notebook and pen. 'Is the convent here in Ceylon?'

'Yes. St Ursula's in Colombo.'

He thanked her and rang off. Mrs Pelham had seemed like a kindly lady. From her description of Rosamund

Collins, she had been far better suited to the Pelham family than to the acerbic Isobel Moncrieff. He went out to the public room. Prasanna and Nadar looked up from their work.

'Good work, you two,' he said. 'I think we've tracked Miss Collins down. She's living in Colombo at St Ursula's convent. I'd like to conduct the interview in person, but it will have to wait until tomorrow. I want to go up to the Moncrieff plantation tonight. I want to have a look around Flint's office.'

'Do you mean follow the money, sir?' asked Prasanna when de Silva had outlined the idea of examining the plantation's accounts that he and Jane had discussed.

'Well done, Sergeant. Yes, that's often where the answer's to be found. I'd like both of you to come with me. Six eyes are better than two, and although I don't plan on being seen, I'm not banking on it that we won't encounter any trouble.'

The telephone rang and Nadar answered it. He listened for a moment then put his hand over the receiver. 'It's Mr Clutterbuck for you, sir.'

'I'll take it in my office.'

'Good afternoon, de Silva.' Archie's voice boomed down the line. 'Anything to report?'

De Silva decided not to mention his plan to go up to the plantation that night. Archie might not agree with the clandestine search. He would fill him in later if he could sweeten the information with a positive result.

'Nothing of importance, sir.' It was true, after a fashion.

'I've been talking with some of my contacts in the motor racing fraternity. It has its uses being president of Nuala's association. Means I know most people involved in the country. One chap remembered that Donald Moncrieff had a crash at a race in Galle.'

De Silva pictured the lovely seaside town, famous for the massive fortifications built by the Portuguese and the

Dutch when they occupied Ceylon.

'Off the top of his head,' Archie continued, 'he couldn't recall the year, but he promised to make a few enquiries and come back to me. I've just heard from him that it was in the autumn of 1923.'

So, if Donald had broken his leg in the crash it was two years before Isobel Moncrieff married his father. She had probably been telling the truth when she said she knew nothing about it.

'Did this gentleman know whether Mr Moncrieff sustained any injuries?'

'I'm afraid not, but if he did, my contact thought he was most likely to have been treated at a private clinic down there. Apparently, there's one that had a very good reputation. Maybe Hebden would have some information on it. I suggest you get in touch with him again.'

'I will, sir. Thank you for your help.'

'Oh by the way, I'm afraid I haven't had time to look into that bank business yet.'

De Silva had almost forgotten he had asked Archie if he would make inquiries into whether money had been going out of Donald Moncrieff's bank accounts.

'But I'll get onto it.'

'Thank you.'

Putting down the receiver, he felt slightly guilty. He hoped that keeping his plan for tonight from Archie wasn't going to backfire. He glanced at his watch. David Hebden might be seeing patients, but he could at least find out when would be a convenient time to call him back.

'The doctor's about to go out on his afternoon house calls,' said the receptionist who answered the surgery telephone. 'But I'll try to catch him for you.'

De Silva waited, listening to the sounds from the street drifting through the half-open window of his office. The customary hum of daily life grew louder as a cow bellowed and voices were raised. He was on the verge of putting his head round the door to the public room and telling Prasanna or Nadar to go and intervene when Hebden came on the line.

'My apologies. I meant to call you, but it's been a busy morning. My receptionist looked out Lucas's notes for me. I have them in front of me now. Can you hold on a moment?'

'Of course.'

'Moncrieff seems to have been a pretty healthy sort of chap,' said Hebden returning. 'Only a couple of visits in all the time he was Lucas's patient. On both occasions, Lucas prescribed painkillers following on from a leg injury. There's a note that the leg was broken in two places as a result of an accident in 1923. It was set at a clinic in Galle. I suppose coincidences can happen, but it looks like we've identified your man.'

'Indeed it does. Many thanks for your help.'

After he'd rung off, de Silva realised he hadn't asked Hebden if he would be able to examine the bones with a view to giving an opinion on the cause of death, but it had waited eight years. Another day or two was unlikely to make a difference.

He looked at his watch. It would soon be dark. He decided to stay on at the station and have something to eat in town before he, Prasanna, and Nadar visited the Moncrieff plantation. If they arrived there mid-evening, it should be a safe bet that Peter Flint would have left his office for the night.

CHAPTER 9

There was still time left before the moon came up, and fortunately it was a cloudy night with only a few stars emerging from amongst the clouds. All the same, de Silva took the precaution of turning off the Morris's headlights not long after he turned off the public road. He drove slowly, his eyes straining to spot any hazards he needed to avoid. Neither he, Prasanna, nor Nadar spoke.

Where the lane divided, he recalled that the way to the plantation buildings and Flint's office lay to the left. He took it and they continued through the dark sea of tea terraces. A little short of the plantation buildings, he pulled the Morris into a layby. Presumably, it had been put there to give cars and other vehicles somewhere to pass the trucks used to haul tea down to the markets and shipping warehouses in Colombo. He parked as close as he dared to the rough ground at its edge, hoping the shadows would partially conceal the Morris. Turning off the engine, he reached into the glove compartment for a torch. Prasanna and Nadar already had theirs in their hands.

'We'll keep to the trees until we're close to the plantation buildings. The office is to the left of the drying area. I noticed it when I came down here with Flint to speak to the workers. Their living quarters are some way off, but I'd be very surprised if there isn't a nightwatchman. We'll have to take care not to attract his attention. Be as quiet as you can. If I give the signal to halt, don't move a muscle.' The young men murmured their assent.

De Silva led the way. They kept their torch beams low, pools of light bobbing like fireflies a few yards ahead of their feet. De Silva stopped a few times, holding up a hand to halt Prasanna and Nadar, but then decided that the noises he heard were nothing more than the grunts and scuffles of nocturnal creatures going about their business.

They had been walking cautiously for several minutes when a susurrating sound made de Silva pause to peer into the tree canopy. An owl settled on a branch and folded its wings, watching them with fierce, unblinking green eyes. Distracted by the sight, de Silva caught his foot under a root and pitched forwards, failing to smother a shout of alarm as he stumbled and saved himself.

'Are you alright, sir?' Prasanna's concerned voice was close to his ear.

He dusted off his trousers. 'Yes,' he muttered irritably. He had lectured his officers on staying quiet and not managed it himself, but with luck they were still far enough away from the buildings for his shout to go unheard. If not, he hoped whoever noticed it would assume it came from a bird or animal.

Another few minutes of careful progress brought them to a spot right by the plantation buildings. Once more, de Silva raised a hand to indicate they should pause. He scanned the buildings for signs of movement and saw none. The area where the freshly picked tea leaves were sorted was about fifty yards away from where they stood. As he had recalled, the office was to its left. He tried to remember if there had been a shack where a watchman might spend the night but couldn't picture one. He would have to hope that any watchman on duty wasn't too close to the office and not due to make his rounds for a while.

The scent of tea filled his nostrils as they padded across

the beaten earth of the sorting yard. Near the doors to the drying room, large paniers full of fresh tea leaves waited to be moved on to that stage of the process. The office loomed out of the darkness: a single-storey building made of corrugated iron. De Silva fished in his pocket for his lock-picking kit. There was only one lock on the door, and it didn't take him long to deal with it. The three men slipped inside, and de Silva relocked the door behind them.

The windows had thin curtains which they drew across to mask some, if not all of the light from their torches. Continuing to keep the beams low, they surveyed the room. There were shelves crammed with files, metal cabinets that presumably held more papers, and a large wooden desk with a swivel chair upholstered in faded red leather behind it. On the desk stood an oil lamp, IN and OUT trays, a pot of pens and pencils, and a box of stationery. There was a locked safe in one corner. He didn't see any bunches of keys, but when he tried the top drawer of one of the metal cabinets, it slid towards him. Good, it would save time if nothing apart from the safe was locked.

They began to search.

'There are some account ledgers in here, sir,' said Prasanna, raising his head from a drawer in one of the metal filing cabinets.

De Silva stopped what he was doing and went to see. 'Let's have them out.'

He switched off his torch and put it on the floor then took a hefty armful of ledgers from Prasanna.

'I'll need a better light to read by, and I don't want these torch beams to be any more visible from the front of the building than they already are.' He jerked his head towards a door on the opposite side of the room to where they had come in. 'See where that leads, Nadar.'

Nadar was soon back. 'It's a storeroom, sir. But there's not much space to spread out,' he added doubtfully.

'It will have to do. Balance my torch on top of these books. I'll go back there and make a start. You two keep searching this room and bring me anything else you think might be relevant.'

The storeroom was indeed cramped, and it was hot and airless. However, it had its own door leading to the outside at the back of the building. He dumped the ledgers on the floor, managed to unlock the door and left it ajar. With some difficulty, he squatted down in a space where he could fit between stacks of crates and boxes. He was grateful that none of his old colleagues were there to see him. If the sight amused Prasanna and Nadar, hopefully they were still sufficiently in awe of their boss not to show it.

The first ledger he opened contained accounts for the year 1926. Isobel Moncrieff had said that her husband died in 1930, so he would still have been in charge then. Time and humidity had faded and browned the ink making it a chore to read, but as he turned the pages, de Silva noted that the business had showed a healthy profit in those days. He worked his way through the rest of the ledgers in the pile. There was nothing later than 1929 and mostly the figures told the same story although profits dipped a little in the last year or so. Presumably, that had been due to Victor Moncrieff's illness.

Painfully, he hauled himself to his feet and poked his head around the door to the office. 'I've finished with these. You can put them back. They only go up to 1929. Have you found some for later years?'

Nadar came to fetch the ledgers. 'Yes, sir. There's more carrying on from then and some bank statements. I'll fetch them for you.'

As he went through the new batch of ledgers and the bank statements, De Silva soon realised that it was a different story from the autumn of 1930 when Donald Moncrieff took over. The plantation's income dwindled, and the amount of money taken out rose.

Prasanna's head appeared around the door. 'Sir!' he whispered urgently. 'I think I can hear someone coming towards the front of the building. What shall we do?'

'We should be safe as long as he stays at the front, but we mustn't be found in here.' He glanced through the open door behind him. In the darkness outside, he made out something that looked like a tall bamboo screen about ten feet wide.

'Put this lot back quickly and try to make it look as if nothing's been disturbed then come in through here and shut the office door. We'll leave by this one and pull it to behind us – quietly, mind.'

He pointed to the screen outside. 'We'll have to hide behind that until he's gone. I need to look through the rest of the ledgers. Thank goodness I locked the main office door behind me. Off you go.'

Once outside and behind the screen, it immediately became apparent what it was put there for. De Silva's nose wrinkled at the smell, but he supposed that rudimentary sanitary arrangements were an inevitable part of a workplace like this. After a few moments, a torch beam wavered around the side of the building. His mouth dry, de Silva felt Nadar stiffen beside him. Presumably, the owner of the torch was the nightwatchman doing his rounds. Were they to be discovered, three uniformed policemen, standing in a row by a latrine on a remote plantation in the middle of the night, would require some explaining.

Fortunately, the nightwatchman didn't try the unlocked storeroom door and walked on to the corner of the building where, to de Silva's dismay, he sat down on a rough stool, his back resting against the corrugated iron wall. Whistling tunelessly, he pulled something from his pocket and put it in his mouth. There was a smell of tobacco, combined with a faint aroma of spices. The man was chewing betel and he looked to be settling down for a while. No doubt this was a regular resting place where he wouldn't be seen shirking his duties.

De Silva shifted his weight from one foot to the other to ease the prickling sensation that had built up. The bamboo screen was not high enough to conceal them unless they stooped a little, or in Prasanna's case a lot, so his back had started to ache as well. He longed to move about more freely, but the chance of the nightwatchman hearing him was too great. How he envied Prasanna and Nadar the flexibility of their young muscles and bones. He tried to concentrate on the beauty of the moonlight as it filtered through the bamboo screen, transforming its humble weave into a thing of patterned, silvery elegance. The warm air pulsed with the throb of insects, punctuated from time to time by a cough from the nightwatchman and the sound of spitting.

After what seemed like hours, but clearly wasn't, the watchman got to his feet. For a moment he hesitated, looking over at the bamboo screen. De Silva tensed; what if he decided to come over to relieve himself? Fortunately, he was either lazy or the possessor of a sensitive nose, for he ambled over to a tree that was much closer to the office and used that instead. As he walked away around the side of the office and out of sight, de Silva allowed himself to straighten up. He pulled his shoulders back and exhaled a long breath. 'Well done, both of you,' he said in an undertone. 'We'll wait a few minutes to be sure he's really gone then get back to the job.'

Back inside the storeroom, another half hour of looking through ledgers didn't change de Silva's impression of the plantation's financial health. It looked like Peter Flint had been telling the truth when he said the business had a long way to go to recover. De Silva had just finished reading the accounts for the previous year when Prasanna came in from the main office. 'We've found a key to the safe, sir. It was taped to the back of a drawer.'

De Silva handed him the previous year's accounts. 'Take these and I'll come and look.'

Inside the safe, there were more account ledgers. De Silva studied them with interest. They covered the period from 1932 up to the present date but showed profits over and above the ones recorded in the ledgers he had already seen. The new profits went into two bank accounts, both of them numbered rather than named. In view of the incriminating nature of it all, he was surprised that Peter Flint had left the key to the safe in his office, but perhaps over time he had grown confident that it wouldn't be discovered. He looked up.

'Excellent work. I think we've found what we need.'

'Do you think Peter Flint's stealing from the business, sir?' asked Prasanna.

'It certainly looks as if that's the case. I'm also considering the possibility that there's something between him and Marina Moncrieff. They may have been siphoning money off to keep it out of her husband's hands.'

The look of concentration on Nadar's face made him supress a smile. 'That would mean they expect him to come back, sir, wouldn't it?' he said at last. 'So they can't be guilty of his murder.'

'Or only one of them thinks he'll return,' said Prasanna.

De Silva nodded. 'Either might be the case. But we still need an explanation for why there are two numbered accounts. Any ideas?'

'Mr Moncrieff's stepmother, sir?' asked Prasanna after a short pause.

'Good. Go on.'

'The second account might be hers, with the first one belonging to Peter Flint and Marina Moncrieff.'

'That leaves us with the question of whether they're all implicated in Donald Moncrieff's murder, or one or more of the three are simply unwitting beneficiaries of it. Now that we've tracked down Isobel Moncrieff's former companion, she may have something revealing to say about the relationship between the four of them.' He yawned. 'We'll take a last look around the office, then we'd better lock up and get out of here before anyone stirs.'

CHAPTER 10

Half an hour later, after checking that everything was back in the place where they had found it, de Silva led the way to the Morris. He was glad that the nightwatchman hadn't proved to be particularly assiduous in his duties. He wouldn't have relished spending any more time hiding in the insalubrious area behind the bamboo screen, still less being found out.

A light breeze had got up. The leaves of the banana trees beyond the clearing swayed gently, making a sound like water trickling over stones. The moon was high now, its ghostly light clearly illuminating their faces. As the Morris came into sight, he felt the sense of relief he always did when leaving her unattended in a remote place. With wild animals at large, especially inquisitive monkeys, one could never be sure. The noise of the engine turning over sounded alarmingly loud in the stillness. A bird shot up out of the undergrowth, squawking indignantly then flapped away into a tree. De Silva's heart thudded. He must have been more apprehensive than he'd realised that their expedition would go awry.

He pulled out of the layby and set off, glad to leave the plantation buildings behind. The Morris's headlights were still off, but in the moonlight he took the risk of driving a little faster than he had on the way down. From the passenger seat beside him, Prasanna watched the road, warning him when he saw potholes. Steady breathing from the back indicated that Nadar had gone to sleep.

They passed a side turning that de Silva had noticed on the way down. He'd known not to take it, but he'd wondered where it went then assumed it was probably an estate road leading to more tea terraces.

A few hundred yards further on, Prasanna leant forward in his seat and stiffened. 'There's something big ahead of us in the middle of the road, sir.'

'Yes, I can just about make it out. A truck? If it is, it's a very large one and out here at an odd time.' He twisted to look back over his shoulder. 'I'll back up to that side turning. I doubt it would be able to pass us, and anyway, I'd rather not be seen. We don't want to have to answer any questions, do we?' *Although it might be a bit late for that*, he thought ruefully. In case they were stopped, he cast about for a plausible explanation of what they were doing at the plantation at such an unearthly hour.

In the dim light, reversing was much harder than driving forwards. He took it slowly, wincing at every bump and scrape on the rough road. A grumbling ache had started in his neck and shoulders. 'How are we doing, Prasanna?'

'Pretty well, sir. It's not coming too fast—' Prasanna broke off and let out a sudden exclamation.

De Silva scowled. 'Don't do that, Sergeant. I need to concentrate.'

'It's not a truck, sir,' said Prasanna in an agitated voice.

'Then what is it?' De Silva braked and turned to look. The shape that had in the distance looked like a single object had divided and spread out to fill the road and a wide strip of land on either side. He saw saplings and bushes bend like grass under it as it moved slowly but inexorably towards the Morris. Behind him, Nadar regained consciousness. 'Elephants, sir!'

'I can see them.'

He put his foot on the accelerator; he'd have to go faster than he'd planned. Right now, the elephants looked to be ambling along steadily, but they might take it into their heads to speed up at any moment. If alarmed, they might charge and the Morris, and quite probably the three of them with her, would have no more chance of escaping unscathed than those saplings.

Despite his best efforts, the Morris veered perilously close to one side of the road. He only just managed to straighten her in time to stop the rear wheel going into the ditch. He glanced at the elephants. They were close now, and he saw that there were eight of them: six adults, one of them a bull, and two young ones. His huge ears flapping, the bull turned to face the Morris. His trunk snaked into the air and he trumpeted. De Silva held his breath. If the bull charged now, there was no hope of avoiding him.

'Should we get out and run, sir?' asked Nadar nervously.

'Not yet.' De Silva went back to edging along the road. He had a theory that with wild animals, it was best to move slowly. Speed was likely to increase their natural inclination to attack anything they saw as a threat.

The bull seemed calmer, but protective still, using his enormous bulk as a barrier between the Morris and his family. He laid his trunk over the back of the female nearest to him. In any other situation, de Silva would have been touched by the display of affection.

Putting a more reassuring distance between the Morris and the elephants, they reached the side turning. De Silva overshot it then turned the Morris in facing forwards. The sky was already lightening in the east and he certainly didn't want to return to the plantation buildings. Equally, unless the elephants moved well out of the way, trying to get past them was madness. He would just have to hope that this track led to somewhere where they could get off the Moncrieffs' land and back to the public road.

As the darkness rapidly retreated, the tea terraces emerged in all their emerald beauty, lush and sparkling after a spell in the cooler air of the night. A thin line of gold appeared on the horizon. In an hour or so, workers would be up and starting their day. It would be most unfortunate if a carload of policemen was stuck in the midst of all the activity with no plausible explanation as to what they were doing there.

The track wound on for about half a mile then they rounded a bend and saw that it dropped down a little slope. At the bottom stood a bungalow. It was a simple building and the scrap of garden dividing it from the track looked untended, but it seemed more substantial than anything that would be used to house the plantation's workers. Perhaps it was where Peter Flint lived.

De Silva groaned softy. If Flint was a good manager, he'd be an early riser too. The thought had no sooner passed through his mind than a light appeared in one of the bungalow's windows and an unseen hand drew back the curtains. Apprehensively, de Silva watched the front door, but to his relief, for the moment it remained closed.

More lights must have been turned on at the back of the house, for a buttery glow seeped around one side of the building.

'Do either of you see somewhere where we can keep out of sight?' he asked. 'I think this is where Flint lives. We might have to wait until he goes off to work. After that, we'll have to hope we can get out of here without being spotted. If anyone sees us, I'll invent some story about coming down to ask him a few more questions and losing the way.' It might be harder to explain why they had chosen such an early hour.

'That tree might hide the car, sir,' said Prasanna, pointing to a large baobab with a thick gnarled trunk to their right.

De Silva smiled. 'You're an optimist, Sergeant, but I can't

see anywhere better.' He released the handbrake and let the Morris roll down the last part of the incline. 'You'd better get out and push,' he muttered when she stopped. 'I'm not starting the engine now. Flint, or whoever lives here, is bound to hear it.'

Prasanna and Nadar put their shoulders to the Morris and she was soon behind the tree. It made a better hiding place than de Silva had thought it would, thanks to some low branches as well as the wide trunk. He motioned to Prasanna and Nadar to get back into the car. 'Now, we wait,' he whispered. 'Let's hope Flint's in a hurry to get to work and not very observant.'

The minutes passed. De Silva pulled his jacket more tightly around him and turned up the collar. He stuffed his hands under his armpits to warm them. If only he had brought gloves and a hat. While they had been occupied with the elephants, he hadn't noticed the dawn chill, but it struck him now how the cold didn't seem to bother Prasanna and Nadar. That was the advantage of young blood and circulation, he thought enviously.

He wondered where Flint kept his car. He'd driven up to the main house the day he'd come to see what was going on, so it must be somewhere. Just then the front door opened, and he tensed. On reflection, if Flint noticed them the best course of action would be to arrest him straight away and question him about the plantation's financial affairs. There was enough evidence that something suspicious was going on to justify it.

He watched as Flint disappeared around the corner of the bungalow then there was the sound of an engine start-ing up. A moment later, his car came into sight. He stopped in front of the bungalow and went inside once more then, after a brief interval, re-emerged. This time there was some-one with him: a woman. She and Flint embraced, then as she moved out of his arms, de Silva recognised her. It was Marina Moncrieff.

He checked that his Webley was ready in case he needed it and quietly got out of the car, motioning Prasanna and Nadar to follow him. They stepped around to the front of the tree and Marina and Flint saw them. She screamed as Flint grabbed her arm and pushed her behind him.

'What the hell do you think you're doing here?' he shouted. 'Don't try anything. I'm armed.'

The shadows under the tree were still quite dense, despite the fact that dawn had broken. De Silva wondered if Flint thought they were thieves. It was unlikely he was expecting a visit from the police at this hour, if at all, so it was a reasonable assumption. It was also a reasonable assumption that out here, Flint would keep a gun to protect himself, but he must take the chance that he didn't have it with him just now. He stepped into the light and levelled his gun at the couple.

'Don't move. You're both under arrest.'

CHAPTER 11

'What a night of it you've had, dear,' said Jane after Shanti had described events at the plantation. 'You must be exhausted.'

'I think I'll try and sleep for a while when I've finished this.' He forked up another mouthful of the omelette their cook had prepared. It was more a mid-morning snack than breakfast.

'What happened after you arrested Marina and Flint?'

'Marina seemed too shocked and distressed to speak and Flint took charge. He insisted that if the remains were those of Donald, then neither of them had anything to do with his death, nor had they suspected that the story of his disappearance might be untrue. But he couldn't deny he was guilty of obstructing the course of justice by refusing to reveal Marina's whereabouts.'

'Did he have a theory about who did kill Donald?'

'He thought it might be one of the people who worked for him. Apparently, he was as unpopular with most of his staff as he was with his family.'

Jane frowned. 'One wonders why any of his workers would take the risk of killing him. What advantage would there be? Why not just leave the plantation?'

'I suppose he could have found out that one of them was stealing from him and threatened them with arrest.'

'Did you believe Flint?'

De Silva rasped a hand over the day-old stubble on his chin. 'I'm not sure. I'll need to question him again when he's had time to reflect on his predicament. Contrary to the way things often happen in detective stories, criminals rarely blurt out a confession the moment they're apprehended.'

'Where are Marina and Flint now?'

'I used the telephone at his office to contact Archie.'

Once more a mental picture of his boss, woken early and coming sleepily to the telephone garbed in dressing gown and pyjamas, rose before de Silva's eyes.

'I wanted to come home,' he went on. 'And I thought it was only fair to give Prasanna and Nadar the chance to get some sleep too. They did a good job last night. Anyway, even though he had to be dragged out of bed, Archie rose to the occasion and sent reinforcements. For now, Flint's locked up at the police station with a couple of the Residence's staff keeping an eye on him. It was harder to know what to do with Marina. In the end I decided the best course was to ask Archie to arrange for her to be taken care of. She's up at the Residence under house arrest. Archie also agreed to see to it that the other stations are contacted and told they can call off the search.'

'I'm not surprised it was all too much for Marina,' said Jane. 'Even though she wasn't happy with her husband, if she's innocent, it must have been an awful shock to hear that he was murdered, and for her and her lover to be accused of it. Her past doesn't seem to have been a happy one, and now her future must look bleak indeed.'

'I agree, although we can't rule out the possibility that she's guilty yet.'

He wiped his mouth and stood up. 'Don't let me sleep for more than a couple of hours. I ought to go to the station and see Flint. Archie may want a word too.'

As he drifted off to sleep, another thing occurred to him. Someone would have to tell Isobel Moncrieff that Marina and Flint had been arrested. He wondered what her reaction would be. If she was involved, would her behaviour betray her? Her self-control seemed to be such that he doubted it, although she had shown some distress when she'd heard that Marina was a suspect. Should he arrest her anyway? That was a knotty problem. Given her status, he had a feeling that it wouldn't go down well with Archie. The situation had been different with Marina. By disappearing, she had brought justifiable suspicion upon herself. And what about Perera? Was it time to rule him out? De Silva fell asleep still very much unsure of where the case was leading.

* * *

He woke just before two o'clock in the afternoon and went to the bathroom. After he had splashed water on his face and run a comb through his hair, he went to find Jane.

She was on the verandah, busy with a new piece of knitting. Billy and Bella were stretched out nearby in a patch of sunshine. As always, they had the knack of finding the perfect spot where the rays would warm their furry little bodies.

'Another gift for Emerald's baby?' he asked with a smile.

She held it up. 'I thought a bonnet might come in useful for keeping warm. Babies tend not to grow much hair until they're a few months old.'

Ruefully, he smoothed his own hair. In the last year or two, he'd noticed that a bald patch had been creeping over the crown of his head. 'And middle-aged detectives lose it.'

Jane laughed. 'Poor dear. Now, I've already eaten, but I expect you'd like some lunch.'

'I would.'

She rang the bell and arranged for food to be brought.

Whilst he ate, he and Jane discussed Isobel Moncrieff.

'You said she disapproved of the way her stepson treated Marina,' said Jane. 'And it was clear she didn't like him personally, but from there to committing murder's a big step. And anyway, how would she do it?'

'There was a photograph of her in her drawing room on a hunting expedition. She looked very at home with a gun.'

'Oh, I'm not saying that a woman wouldn't be capable of shooting someone, but you didn't see any evidence of a bullet wound.'

'That's true, but Isobel might have made a clean shot without hitting bone.'

'For that, I think she would have needed to be lucky as well as skilful. But there are plenty of other methods a woman might employ. Poison, for example. Isobel told you that Marina had medical training, so there's a good chance she would have been able to obtain the means to kill Donald.'

'Hmm. And poison would be undetectable now.'

'What about disposing of the body?'

'I doubt either Isobel or Marina would be strong enough, but Peter Flint would.' De Silva thought of those muscular arms. 'Maybe he told the truth when he said that he didn't kill Donald, but he might have helped either of the women to cover up their crime.'

'Or even both of them, if they were all in league to get rid of him.'

De Silva's mouthful of curried green beans suddenly seemed less tasty. 'We still have a long way to go before we uncover the truth,' he said gloomily. 'I doubt it's going to be easy to extract any confessions. Isobel is a strong character, and Peter Flint seems to be no shrinking rosebud.'

'Violet, dear.'

'Ah.'

He pondered for a moment. 'At one time, I thought Marina was the most likely of the three to buckle under

COLD CASE IN NUALA

questioning, but now I'm not so sure. Archie may also present a problem. He seems very co-operative at the moment, and Charlie Frobisher believes he's keen to make amends for the mistakes of the past, but he backed off from questioning Marina before and may do so again. If I'm honest, I don't relish the prospect myself.'

Jane sighed. 'That's understandable. Particularly if she's innocent and suffered as badly at her husband's hands as we've heard.'

She glanced at the empty serving dishes and de Silva's clean plate. 'You were hungry. Shall I ring for more of anything?'

He finished his glass of water. 'No, I'd better be off.'

He came around to her side of the table and kissed her cheek. 'I hope to come home at a sensible time tonight, whatever happens.'

'I hope so too,' said Jane with a smile.

CHAPTER 12

At the station, the two servants Archie had sent down from the Residence were talking quietly together when he came in. They stood to attention.

'How has the prisoner been?' he asked.

'He has given us no trouble, sahib,' said the elder man. 'We fetched food for him this morning, but he has not eaten much.'

'Well done. I'll talk to him now. I'd like you to stay here until my officers arrive. I hope they won't be long.'

The men nodded.

Peter Flint lay on the narrow bed in his cell, his eyes fixed on the ceiling. He turned his head at the rattle of de Silva's key in the lock.

'Hello, Inspector. I've been wondering when you'd arrive.'

De Silva closed the metal grille and relocked it. The air in the cell was stale and the smell of curry lingered. A meagre ray of sunshine fell from a high, barred window, supplementing the dim light coming from the corridor. The cell faced north, and the lower parts of the bars were green with lichen.

He sat down on the hard chair facing the bed. Flint didn't move.

'I hope the time to reflect on your situation has been useful, Mr Flint. Are you ready to tell me the truth now? It's sure to come out in the end, and it may make things easier for you if you're honest with me. I should also tell you that I have searched your office and am aware that you have been keeping two sets of financial accounts and have been making substantial payments to anonymous bank accounts. Basically, you have been hiding secret profits. I assume you have benefitted, and you need to tell me who else has.'

'What makes you so sure that I wasn't telling the truth last night?'

'My instinct for detecting when someone is lying has served me well over the years.'

There was a long pause. De Silva waited.

'If I tell you everything, I want your assurance that nothing will happen to Marina. She's the innocent party in all this.'

'You know as well as I do, that I can't promise you anything at this stage. The only assurance I can give you is that whatever happens, she'll receive a fair trial.'

The expression on Peter Flint's face darkened and his eyes narrowed. 'I suppose that's the best we can hope for,' he muttered. Another silence ensued. Deciding to let Flint take his time, de Silva took his notebook out of his breast pocket.

'Alright, I'll tell you what happened,' said Flint at last. 'It was two days after the 1932 rally took place. I was in my office late, finishing off some paperwork. It was getting dark, so I went outside to find oil for my desk lamp. The servant who normally filled it must have forgotten to do so that morning. I made a mental note to reprimand him. I was on the point of going back inside when Moncrieff came around the corner. I saw from the way he carried himself that he was in the mood for a fight. It was likely the workers had gone to their huts, but there might have been a few stragglers. Bad for morale to see the bosses arguing, so I suggested we go into the office and deal with whatever he wanted to talk about in private. He made some grudging comment, but he agreed.'

There was another pause. De Silva speculated whether it was because after eight years Flint was having to think hard to recollect the exact sequence of events, or because he was constructing his story as he went along. For the moment, he reserved judgment.

'Once we were in the office, I waited for Moncrieff to begin. More than once, I'd seen him when he lost control, and I hoped silence on my part would be the best way to keep him calm. But it soon became clear that very little I could say or leave unsaid was going to defuse the situation. He started on about how he knew Marina and I had become involved and that I'd been trying to turn her against him from the start.'

Flint smiled bitterly. 'That wouldn't be a difficult task, believe me, although I swear on my honour it wasn't something that I deliberately set out to do. The affection between us grew slowly, and I think we both tried to resist it at first. For my part, that was because I knew the danger that she was likely to face from Moncrieff if he found out she was unfaithful. There was also the prospect of her being shunned by the British community.' He scowled. 'Even though she's worth ten of most of them, people can be such hypocrites. As far as Marina was concerned, I'm sure she had scruples about breaking her marriage vows, even though much later she told me that she'd made up her mind about it being the right thing for us to be together far sooner than I did.'

He seemed lost in thought for a while. De Silva heard a noise above him and glanced up to see that a blue magpie had landed on the sill of the barred window. It pecked insistently at the lichen then flew away in a flash of indigo and white. He shifted on the uncomfortable chair. 'What happened next?'

'He started to insult me. Although he'd never had to work for his money and was reckless with what he'd been given into the bargain, Moncrieff liked to give the impression that he was a bigshot in business. He told me I was a fool to think that a no-hoper like me could ever be more to Marina than a temporary amusement. She was bored at the plantation and I was a novelty, but she'd soon tire of me. And that would happen even sooner than it might have done because he was firing me, and he'd make sure I didn't get another job in the Hill Country. Marina would certainly have no time for a man with no job, no money, and no prospects. He started to make allegations against her, claiming this wasn't the first time she'd been unfaithful. I was sure it wasn't true. She'd sworn to me there'd been no one else.'

Flint pushed his hair out of his eyes; there were beads of sweat on his forehead and damp patches on his shirt under the armpits. His voice had become croaky.

'Would you like some water, Mr Flint?'

'Moncrieff just laughed when I told him that,' said Flint, seeming not to hear the question. 'He told me that if I believed the word of a tramp, I was more of a fool than he'd thought I was. I was a fool in one way for sure,' he added sourly. 'And that was to let him get to me. It was the way he talked about Marina, sneering at her when I knew what she'd suffered at his hands, that made me snap. I couldn't stay in my seat. I knew that if it was the last thing I did, I had to wipe that self-satisfied look off his face. I got up, went around to his side of the desk, and grabbed him by the collar. I don't think he was expecting it because I had him off his feet with no difficulty.'

Flint clenched his fists and de Silva saw the muscles in his arms bulge. From the photographs of Donald Moncrieff, he'd been a big man but probably not as fit, and certainly not as young, as his manager.

'He recovered soon enough and lashed out at me. The punch caught me off balance and I toppled backwards against the desk. My spine must have hit a sharp edge of wood because I felt a stab of pain.' Flint's lips drew back, baring strong white teeth. 'Then I went for him.'

With a jolt, de Silva sensed what a formidable opponent the manager would be. He was glad he'd had the backup of Prasanna and Nadar in case he'd needed it.

'Everything's a little hazy after that,' Flint continued. 'All I'm certain of is that I didn't intend to kill Moncrieff. I just wanted him to feel some of the pain Marina had suffered and to know that his time for tormenting her was over. I punched him and he started to bleed from his nose. It was as if the sight of the blood made me even angrier. I think I would have gone on hitting him if he hadn't managed to break free. He lunged for the oil lamp on my desk and knocked it over. Luckily, the glass didn't shatter, and I managed to right it before anything caught alight, but it gave Moncrieff his chance to get as far as the door. I wasn't prepared to let him escape though. I was worried he'd go after Marina.'

'What did you intend to do after you'd stopped him?' asked de Silva quietly.

Flint exhaled a long sigh. 'I don't think I'd got any further than wanting to stop him. I grabbed him by the shoulder, and he swung around and tried to punch me again, but I was faster than he was. He fell awkwardly, knocking the back of his head hard on the edge of the metal cabinet nearby. There was more blood from his nose and now some coming out of his ear. He just looked at me, an expression, if anything, of surprise on his face, then he slumped to the floor.'

Flint gave de Silva a sideways glance. Was he trying to gauge how the story was going down? It crossed de Silva's mind that he still hadn't asked Hebden to check over the bones. Surely a blow such as Flint described would cause a fracture to Moncrieff's skull? If Hebden didn't find one, it might be proof Flint was lying.

'I've always kept a spare shirt at the office to change

into if the one I start the day in gets too damp and filthy to be pleasant,' Flint went on. 'I balled it up and tried to stop the bleeding with it, but the blood just kept coming through. Moncrieff's eyes were closed, and he didn't open them when I splashed water from the jug on my desk over his face. I was still wary though. I knew he was crafty. He might really be conscious and planning to go for me again when he thought I was least ready for him.'

Flint shivered, wrapping his arms around his chest. 'It wasn't until his skin started to feel clammy and I saw a grey tinge around his lips that I began to be afraid he really was in a bad way. I panicked and tried to pump his chest. There was even a moment when I thought I was getting somewhere, but looking back, I should have called for help. The telephone was right there, but I hesitated. It would be his word against mine over who'd started the fight. I already knew my job was gone but finding another one would be hard enough with no references, probably impossible with a conviction for assaulting my boss on my record.'

A look of misery came over his face. 'I wasn't sure how Marina would react either. Later, when my head was clear again, I was sure he'd lied about her seeing other men, but I'm ashamed to say that in the heat of the moment, his accusations shook my faith in her. Was he right about what I meant to her? Would she stand by me, or would I lose her too?'

There were footsteps in the corridor. De Silva looked up to see Prasanna. He wished his sergeant hadn't interrupted them. The intrusion had broken the flow of Flint's confession, but it was too late.

'Nadar is back as well, sir,' said Prasanna. 'Shall I tell the staff from the Residence they may go?'

'Yes, tell them to give a message to Mr Clutterbuck that I'll be in touch with him later.'

He waited for the sound of Prasanna's footsteps to die away before prompting Flint to go on.

'When did you realise that Donald Moncrieff was dead?'

'A few minutes later maybe. No, I can't say for sure. It seemed like hours. In my job, I'd often been called upon to shoot animals, both the wild and the domestic variety. I'm not afraid of the sight of blood, but this was something different. I felt sickened.'

He raised his head and looked wretchedly at de Silva. 'A man's life gone… I knew that by losing my temper I had probably changed my own for ever as well. And Marina's, if she still wanted me. What are those lines about mercy dropping like the gentle rain from heaven? It was going to take a deluge to save me. If people found out about us, they'd never believe I was innocent.'

The manager was one of the last people he would have expected to quote Shakespeare, thought de Silva. Odd how people had the power to surprise one.

'The enormity of what I'd done horrified me,' Flint went on. 'I decided my only chance was to conceal what had happened. Marina told me that she and Donald hadn't shared a bedroom for many months. When she went down to breakfast that morning, she wasn't particularly surprised to find him not at home. Although even for him such a sudden departure was unusual, it wasn't completely out of character. A few days later, Colonel McTaggart came sniffing around, then Archie Clutterbuck became involved. I carried on with my work and kept my head down. Then I heard that Isobel's companion, Miss Collins, claimed to have heard Donald making plans to leave with some woman of his and I blessed providence for intervening on my side. I'd no idea who the woman was or what happened to her, but it didn't matter. She was my saviour.'

Flint's story was plausible, but it didn't explain everything. De Silva still wasn't sure he believed him. 'How did you move Moncrieff's body to the place where you buried it?'

Briefly, Flint looked startled at the question then recovered. 'I hauled him into the back of the jeep he drove down to see me in − it was the one he used to get around the plantation − and covered him with a rug.'

'Why that particular patch of ground? Why not somewhere nearer to your office?'

'I didn't want to run the risk of being seen if I buried him near the office or the drying sheds and the best place I could think of that was both accessible and private and would take me the least time, was behind the courtyard at the main house. In the darkness, anyone looking out of the window would see the jeep drive through the archway and away into the courtyard and assume it was Donald driving it.'

'What happened to the Bugatti?' He deliberately sprang the question on Flint to see how he reacted.

'The Bugatti? Of… of course, I knew I had to find a way of making it look as if Moncrieff had taken it with him. After I'd buried the body, I left the jeep in the courtyard and got the Bugatti out of the garage. Moncrieff and I weren't too dissimilar in build and as luck would have it, he'd left a cap in the car. I wore it as I drove the Bugatti back through the archway. I hoped that if anyone saw me, they would assume it was Moncrieff going for a spin or taking off to impress one of his lady friends. As it happened, I needn't have worried as it seemed no one actually saw me coming back in the jeep or leaving in the Bugatti. I hid it in one of the outhouses at my bungalow and, over time, I dismantled it. I burned what I could, broke up the rest and dumped it. I wasn't afraid of anyone thinking to search my property as everyone assumed Moncrieff was still very much alive, as I intended.'

If that was true, de Silva winced at the thought of the desecration of such a beautiful car.

'I expect you want to know where Marina stands in all this,' said Flint. 'I swear that I've never told her what happened that night. She believed her husband left her for another woman. I didn't involve her or anyone else in disposing of the body or the car. For several months after that, Marina had nightmares about Donald coming back. I was tempted more than once to assure her that at last she was safe, but I forced myself not to. I didn't want to put her in a compromising position.'

'What about Mr Moncrieff's stepmother?'

'Isobel? I've never entirely fathomed what goes on in her head. She asked a few questions but quickly seemed to assume that he'd absconded.' He laughed. 'A practical lady, Isobel. It wasn't long before our conversations only concerned the financial side of the situation.'

He paused and wiped a hand across his lips. 'It's stifling in here. I'll have that water now.'

De Silva went to the door and called out. Shortly afterwards, Nadar appeared.

'Bring Mr Flint a glass of water.'

They waited in silence for it to arrive. Flint gulped it down before resuming. 'She told me that she had no need of money herself, but she was concerned that if Moncrieff came back, he'd squander the plantation's profits as he'd done in the past and the business would suffer. She also suggested this was an opportunity to make some of the improvements that he had resisted and keep the cost quiet. I can't claim I went along with her ideas purely for those reasons. I was also swayed by her offer that some of the profit we hid should go to Marina and me.' He smiled wryly. 'You've seen the evidence as to how I did it. A kind of running away fund if you like. In any case, as you may have noticed, not many people oppose Isobel for long.'

De Silva pictured the scene. Isobel would no doubt have made good use of her imperious manner. He wondered if there'd also been a lingering anxiety in Flint's mind that influenced his actions. Did she believe the story that her stepson had simply disappeared quite as wholeheartedly as she appeared to on the surface? Wasn't it safer to accommodate her rather than risk her insisting on tracing him? After all, the plantation was in her family. She might not have been entirely happy to place her trust in Flint, a man she'd not known for long. Particularly once she knew of the feelings that he and Marina had for each other.

'In any case, she set out her requirements.'

It sounded a cold transaction. That didn't surprise de Silva.

'If I fell in with the plan, there'd be no questions asked. Provided I continued to run the plantation, and saw to it that the profits held up, Marina I and were welcome to please ourselves.'

De Silva frowned. Flint wouldn't be the first man to close his mind to inconvenient matters. Archie was a case in point. Why rock the boat?

'Returning to the present, on the night Mr Moncrieff's remains were discovered, where were you?'

'At my bungalow. Marina was with me. She often stayed. The main house holds many unhappy memories for her, so she's always preferred to spend as little time there as possible.'

De Silva thought of Muttu. Presumably, the servant had lied and knew perfectly well where Marina was likely to be. It was hard to blame him though. He would have been hampered by loyalty to his employer.

'When were you aware that the remains had been found?'

'Muttu telephoned me after you saw him that night and told him about it. He was in a terrible state. Thought he was to blame somehow but I told him to stay calm and just keep denying he knew where Marina was. She was already asleep, and I didn't wake her. I wanted time on my own to think.' He scowled. 'If it hadn't been for that damned dog, none of this would have happened.'

'I think that will do for now, Mr Flint.' With relief, de Silva eased his backside off the chair. It had begun to feel like a bed of nails.

'What happens now?' asked Flint despondently.

'One of my officers will type up my notes. You'll be given a chance to read them over and dispute anything you believe to be inaccurate. After that, you'll remain in custody until your case is put before a magistrate.'

* * *

On the way back from the cells to his office he gave Nadar his instructions, also telling him to put in a call to the Residence. It was probably time he brought Archie up to date.

The telephone rang on his desk a few minutes later.

'Mr Clutterbuck is out, sir,' said Nadar. 'Do you want to leave a message?'

'Just ask them to say I called and will try again later.' He put down the receiver. In the meantime he'd go back to the plantation and take a good look around Peter Flint's bungalow. Hopefully, it would help him to get a clearer measure of the man.

As he drove away from the station, he saw the Residence's official car coming towards him, its sleek, black paintwork gleaming in the sunshine. If Archie was on board, the middle of the street was not the ideal place for a discussion, but when the car slowed and the rear window rolled down, it was Florence who peered out from the shadowy interior. A waft of perfume and scented face powder drifted towards him on the hot air.

'Good afternoon, Inspector de Silva. How fortunate. I've been wanting a word about Marina Moncrieff.' Florence lowered her voice. 'One doesn't wish to be inhospitable, but it would be helpful to know how much longer you want her to stay at the Residence. It is a rather unusual situation.' She raised a hand to pat a stray hair back into place and her rings caught the light. 'I like to think of the Residence as our home,' she said with a frown. 'Not an outpost of the Tower of London.'

'I'm sorry that you are being inconvenienced, ma'am. I hope it won't need to be for too much longer.'

Florence's expression softened. 'I appreciate it's not entirely your fault. Archibald told me he made the offer. The poor lady arrived in nothing but the clothes she stood up in. This morning I sent one of the maids in a rickshaw to fetch a few things for her.'

'I'm sure she appreciates your kindness.'

'One does one's best, but it's hard to know how to treat someone in her situation. Will she really be charged with murder?'

'Nothing is certain at the moment, ma'am.'

Florence pursed her lips. 'Well, I hope I shan't be the last to be told what is going on.'

'As soon as the situation is clear, you will be first in the line,' said de Silva feeling a little contrite. Even in a house the size of the Residence, there must be some awkwardness in having a guest like Marina.

Two little boys who had been watching the car had sidled close. Out of the corner of his eye, de Silva saw that they were larking around, pulling faces, and giggling at their reflections in one of the car's glossy wheel arches. Florence threw them a quelling glance and they ran away.

'Well,' she said, 'I must be going. I'm already late for my appointment.' The window rolled back up.

As he left the town behind him, de Silva let the needle

on the speedometer climb. He wanted to reach Flint's bungalow while there was still some light.

CHAPTER 13

Out at the plantation, a servant answered the door of Flint's bungalow, his eyes widening when he saw de Silva.

'My master is not here, sahib,' he said anxiously.

De Silva felt sorry for him, then thought of the plantation workers too. He ought to find out if Flint had a second-in-command who would be able to take over the day-to-day management of the place. There were sure to be things that needed doing such as workers' wages to pay and orders to fulfil.

'I know. He's at the police station helping us with some inquiries. You may carry on with your duties while I look around.'

Although the bungalow had not been much to look at from outside, its interior was airy and charming. De Silva wondered if the bright fabrics, comfortable chairs, and well-polished furniture were Marina's touch. Peter Flint had struck him as too much of an outdoor type to be all that interested in creature comforts. But there were other things that interested him. In particular, a fine collection of seashells arranged in a shallow display cabinet caught his eye.

He picked up one that he recognised to be from a black-lipped pearl oyster. It was a beautiful thing; its frilled shell, shading from slate grey to canary yellow, fitted snugly in his hand. He rubbed the pad of his thumb over the gritty outer surface. Inside, the shell was smooth and iridescent, veined and mottled in delicate shades of blue and gold like shallow water in the evening sun. There were also leopard-patterned cowries, gaudily striped cone shells, and shells with strange, bony tentacles that made them look like petrified spiders. He put one of them to his nostrils and inhaled a memory of the sea. It was one of the smells that reminded him of his childhood in Colombo. He had loved the days when his father and mother took him to the beach: the golden sand soft beneath his toes, and the warm sea lapping at his skin. His father taught him to swim but his mother had hated getting wet and ran away shrieking if a surge of foam caught her unawares. He doubted, however, that these shells came from the city's beaches. For years those had been well combed by men looking for something to sell to tourists. Most likely these ones had been collected at one of the wilder places elsewhere on the coast. He and Jane had often said they would visit some of them one day.

His attention turned to the pictures on the walls. They were very different to the kind of thing that he'd seen in the Residence and the other British homes he'd been into. No misty watercolours of picturesque cottages and gardens, no paintings of the British Houses of Parliament and Big Ben, no hunting prints, and no gloomy lakes and castles. Whoever had chosen these pictures had picked out local scenes of people and animals that were rendered with vibrant energy and colour. In one picture, a snarling tiger's orange and black stripes seared his eyes. Beside it, a pen and ink study of an elephant evoked the creature's power so strongly that for a moment his alarm from the previous night's close shave welled up once again. Whoever the artist was, he had an enviable ability to bring his work to life. De Silva peered at the signature and saw that it was Peter Flint's. Another side to the man he wouldn't have predicted.

'Your master is interested in animals,' he said to the servant who had reappeared.

'Yes, sahib.'

The man sounded uninterested. De Silva guessed he had been brought up in one of the villages. Villagers were apt to view wild animals as a threat to their livelihood rather than something to be studied and admired. Tigers ate your goats and cattle; elephants trampled the crops that you had toiled to coax from the earth. For most villagers, life was a struggle to scrape an existence. Their lives had hardly changed from those of their ancestors.

He turned away from the pictures. This wasn't a time for thinking about the way people lived. He knew he was putting off finishing his search and going on to his next task, visiting Isobel Moncrieff. He had to admit that something about her made him feel that the years had fallen away, and he was once more a nervous police cadet. It was a sensation that even Florence at her most imperious failed to inspire to quite such a degree, but then he'd had many years to grow accustomed to Florence.

The rest of the rooms didn't take him long to search. It was clear from the clothes and toiletries in the main bedroom that Marina Moncrieff was at home in the bungalow. Did she avoid the one she had shared with her husband because it held unhappy memories or were there more sinister associations that she wanted to stay buried deep?

A cough reminded him that the servant was still present.

De Silva turned to him. 'I'm finished here. I want you to lock the doors after me. If anyone else comes, you are not to let them in, do you understand? Just find out their name then call one of these numbers. Ask to speak to Inspector de Silva.'

Quickly, he tore a piece of paper out of his notebook and wrote down the numbers of the station and Sunnybank. With a nod, the servant took them.

The sun was low on the horizon, filling the sky with a fiery glow as he walked back to the Morris. It had dimmed to opalescent pink and lilac by the time he turned into the entrance to Isobel's bungalow. Lights already shone in the windows. He stopped the car and got out, straightening his spine, and lifting his chin. It occurred to him that Isobel might already know that Marina and Peter Flint had been arrested. Some, if not all, of the servants at the main house would probably have heard that a maid from the Residence had come to fetch clothes for Marina. He found it hard to credit that none of them had been sufficiently curious to ask what was going on.

* * *

It was the servant, Jamis, who answered the door. His expression was as impassive as it had been on de Silva's first visit. He left de Silva waiting in the hall while he went to tell Isobel she had a visitor. A few moments later, he returned and showed him into the drawing room.

De Silva was glad to find that despite his forebodings, the elegant drawing room and its occupant seemed less intimidating the second time around. Isobel was dressed in a stylish black dress that reached to her ankles. The drop-waisted bodice glittered with jet bugle beads. She wore a triple-stranded pearl choker and a matching bracelet. He wondered if she was expecting guests.

She greeted him with a wan smile. 'I suppose you've come to confirm what I've already gathered from my servant. It's shocking news. I hope Marina is being well looked after. I find it impossible to believe that she knew anything about Donald's death. That is if you're quite sure that they are his remains you've found.'

'I'm afraid there's no doubt, ma'am. As for Mrs Moncrieff, she's perfectly safe. Mrs Clutterbuck has seen to it that she's made comfortable at the Residence.'

Isobel raised an eyebrow. 'How kind. Do you have more to tell me? Muttu's message was that Peter Flint had also been arrested but gave no details of what he was charged with. Is he suspected of murder?'

'He's confessed to having a fight with your stepson on the night he died, but he claims his death was the result of an accident.'

'I see. Did he elaborate on that?'

She listened while de Silva explained the events as Peter Flint had recounted them. When he had finished, she leant forward in her chair. Her expression was grave. 'He's in a perilous situation, isn't he, Inspector?'

'I'm afraid so, ma'am. Since no one else was present when the fight took place, we only have his word as to what happened.'

'Do you think there's a danger he'll be charged with murder? I've known for some time that he and Marina have become close. She deserves some happiness. It would be too cruel if it was snatched away.'

She frowned. 'I want Flint to have the best lawyers available. If necessary, I'll pay for them. What will happen to Marina?'

'For the moment, she'll stay at the Residence under house arrest.'

'I see.'

'How much do you know about Peter Flint, ma'am?'

Isobel gave him a sharp look. 'If you mean do I think him capable of murder, the answer is no. Donald had a violent temper. Plenty of people will attest to that. If they fought, I'm confident that most, if not all, of the provocation would have been on his side and it's true his death was an accident.'

'When did you first meet Mr Flint?'

'When he first came to the plantation. I believe before that he managed a smaller one to the north of here. I had nothing to do with employing him. That was my late husband's decision when his health became too poor for him to cope alone.'

'I understand that when your stepson took over, you had concerns about the way he ran the business.'

'Who told you that?'

'Peter Flint.'

De Silva studied her expression; there was no hint of uneasiness in it. 'He also told me about the arrangement the two of you came to.'

Isobel regarded him calmly. 'Shall we get to the point? I had no qualms about it at the time and I still don't. Holding money in reserve was for the good of the plantation, not for my personal gain. You can't imagine how galling it was for me to see the work that my late husband put into the business wasted. I believed there was a chance that Donald would come back and return to his bad ways. If he had done, I would have done my best to continue the practice, and while he remained absent it was the sensible thing to do. Even unwittingly, he would have benefitted from the improvements Peter brought about in his absence.'

De Silva felt some sympathy for her. If he had been in her position, he would have felt the same.

'I'd be extremely surprised if Donald left me anything in his will,' she went on. 'There was no love lost between us. I assume Marina will inherit the plantation and everything that goes with it.' She looked around her. 'I've grown very fond of this place and would be sorry to leave it. I'm sure she and I can come to an arrangement, but I won't trouble her with business matters at such a difficult time. Now, do you have any more questions for me?'

De Silva stifled his annoyance at her abrupt tone. The

interview had gone no worse than he'd expected, and he'd had a chance to observe Isobel more closely. He was prepared to let her have the satisfaction of being the one to end it.

'No, ma'am. Thank you for your time.'

'Good. Remember, I must be kept informed.'

She reached for the bell on the small table at her elbow and rang it. As they waited for Jamis to come, de Silva noticed that the drawing room's gold silk curtains hadn't been drawn and the double doors between the two windows stood ajar. He recalled from his previous visit that they had appeared to lead straight into the garden rather than to a verandah.

'Is your mistress expecting guests this evening?' he asked as Jamis showed him out.

The servant shook his head. 'The memsahib always dresses for dinner.'

Outside, for Jamis's benefit if he was still watching, de Silva drove a little way down the drive to a point where he was out of sight of the bungalow then stopped. If he returned to it in secret, he might hear something useful. Keeping to the shadows, he made his way back and followed the path that led to the left-hand side of the building. Passing a screen of small trees with an undergrowth of shrubs, he reached the rear garden and crept close to the drawing room doors.

Isobel was still there and Jamis was with her. She was talking to him but in such a low tone that, strain as he might, de Silva was unable to hear what was being said. Was the conversation mundane, or did it have a bearing on the case?

What he did hear clearly was the hum of a mosquito. As quietly as possible, he swatted it away, then pushing aside a low branch of an oleander that partially obstructed his view of the room, he saw Jamis coming towards the doors.

As he reached them, the humming sound began again. The dratted mosquito was back, this time homing in on his neck. Unable to restrain himself, he swatted it again and to his dismay, Jamis paused. De Silva held his breath, praying the servant wouldn't step outside. If he didn't move a muscle, the fellow might think all he'd heard was a lizard snapping up the insect. His heartbeat thudded as Jamis's hand reached out, so close he could have touched it. What seemed like an eternity passed, then he heard Isobel speak. The doors were pulled shut and there was the click of a key turning the lock. The curtains closed, leaving him alone in the darkness.

He waited a few moments then headed back towards the drive and the Morris. He had almost reached the front of the bungalow when he saw a beam of light and heard men's voices seemingly coming in his direction. He froze, edging into the cover of the trees, and waited in the shadows. The men paused quite close by, but although he managed to catch a few words of what was being said, he didn't understand the gist of the conversation. He recognised by his voice, however, that one of them was Jamis. He wasn't sure who the other man was, possibly a nightwatchman.

Eventually they must have moved on for the voices faded, but he decided to go deeper into the trees to get back to the Morris. That way, there was less likelihood of anyone noticing him, and if they thought they saw movement, hopefully they would dismiss it as being caused by an animal.

The sky was clear, and the tree canopy not very dense, so moonlight helped him to see his way. All the same, as he negotiated the rough ground and tangled vegetation with great caution, he was mindful of how easy it would be to lose his way. After a few minutes he reached a place where the trees thinned out and saw a wooden building ahead of him. It was single-storey and big enough for a double garage. He wondered what it was doing there. There appeared to be no obvious route by which one could bring a vehicle up to it, so it was presumably some kind of storage shed. The wide double doors were secured by a heavy, padlocked chain. It was probably not important, but if he came this way again, it might be worth trying to have a look inside.

It was a relief when he found the Morris. Deliberately, he had left her at a place where there was a slight slope to the drive. He engaged neutral then released the handbrake and let her coast until he was well out of earshot before he started the engine.

It occurred to him that he'd done nothing more about Muttu. It was hard to credit he had been telling the truth about Marina when she'd not even left the plantation. Before he returned to Nuala, he ought to find him and caution him severely against telling any more lies.

* * *

There were no lights on at the main house. From the depths of the garden he heard the grunts and snuffles of nocturnal creatures and the low throb of insects. At the front door, he rang the bell, but no one came to answer it. The servants might have gone to their quarters for the night, particularly as there was presumably no one who required dinner to be served to them. He thought of Isobel Moncrieff dining alone in her finery. There was something immeasurably sad about the idea.

He rang a second time but still no one came. Surely, the place wasn't completely deserted. One might expect a senior member of staff like Muttu to be given a room somewhere in the house, or if nothing else, there ought to be a nightwatchman on duty. He went back to the Morris and fetched his torch. The beam bobbed ahead of him as he circled the building, calling out as he went. The last thing he wanted was to be mistaken for an intruder and attacked. Finally, he saw the wavering glow of a lantern and heard a voice. 'Who are you?'

A thick-set man emerged from the gloom. He had a stout stick in one hand and from his suspicious expression, he was prepared to use it.

'I am Inspector de Silva of the Nuala police,' said de Silva hastily, putting a hand to his badge and tilting it so that it caught the light. The nightwatchman's expression relaxed a little. 'I am sorry, sahib. It is very dark tonight.'

'No matter. You are right to be wary. Are you alone at the house?'

'I think all the servants have gone to the huts.'

'Even Muttu?' De Silva frowned.

'Muttu is not here.'

'Do you know where he's gone?'

The nightwatchman shrugged. 'Maybe one of the servants will know. Shall I take you to speak with them?'

'Please.'

De Silva followed him down a track that led away from the house. In the torchlight, he saw a huddle of small huts ahead of them, and as they drew closer, he noticed that the land on either side of the track was cultivated. A variety of scents hung in the warm night air, from the spicy aroma of coriander and curry leaf to the earthy smell of cauliflowers and potatoes. A rumble in his stomach reminded him that dinner time was imminent. He also remembered he had promised Jane he wouldn't be late. Hopefully, he had enough interesting news for her to make up for it.

Stacked up against a wall of the nearest hut were piles of coconuts, small logs, and kindling. He smelled woodsmoke, frying onions, and the sweet, milky scent of simmering rice. Outside the first hut they came to, a woman who was stirring something in a small pan over a fire gave them a startled look. De Silva became aware that other eyes were watching from the shadows as people noticed them and stopped what they were doing, their faces ruddy in the glow of other small fires.

'Who is Muttu's deputy?' he asked the nightwatchman.

'Velu.'

'Point him out to me.'

The watchman peered into the gloom then jabbed a finger at a tall man who watched them from the door of a slightly larger hut than the rest. De Silva went over to him.

'Are you Velu?'

The man waggled his head.

'I came to see Muttu. Can you tell me where I'll find him?'

Velu's face cracked in a smile, revealing a set of crooked, betel-stained teeth. 'I am sorry, sahib, I cannot help you. Maybe he has gone to his village.'

De Silva frowned. 'Why is that?'

'I think maybe one of his family is sick.'

'Did he say when he expected to be back?'

'No, sahib.'

'This village of his, is it far away?'

'I cannot say, sahib. He has not spoken to me about it.'

How convenient of Muttu's relation to be suddenly taken ill, thought de Silva sceptically. There must be hundreds of villages out in the countryside. The chances of finding the one Muttu had fled to were so small as to be almost impossible. Unless he turned up of his own accord, he would probably have to be written off. It wouldn't be the first time he'd come across a servant whose reaction to trouble had been to leave their old life behind them like a snake sloughing off its skin. He didn't always blame them. No doubt the forces of law and order seemed particularly threatening to people in their position.

CHAPTER 14

Back in Nuala, he stopped at the police station to arrange for Prasanna and Nadar to take turns to be in charge of Flint overnight and in the morning.

'How has he been since I left?' he asked. It was not uncommon for men in Flint's situation to attempt to harm themselves.

'We checked on him every hour as you wanted, sir,' said Prasanna. 'He's just been lying on the bed. He seems very calm.'

Was that because he had got his story off his chest and was confident that he would be believed? De Silva found it hard to credit that he wasn't man of the world enough to know that he was in a very precarious position. However good the lawyers Isobel proposed to engage, a jury would only have his word for it that he had not intended to kill Moncrieff or cause him serious harm. He might claim that Moncrieff had provoked the fight, but the fact that he'd had time to call for help and not done so would count against him. Then there was the matter of concealing Marina's whereabouts from the police. He would be very lucky to be found innocent on all counts.

'Nadar, you may as well take the first shift. Prasanna, go and buy some food in the bazaar and bring it back here before you set off for home. After that, be back here by seven tomorrow morning to relieve Nadar. I'm going home now. Nadar, would you telephone my wife, please and tell her I'm on the way.'

* * *

'Am I in trouble?' he asked Bella as he picked her up. She had been waiting for him by the front door. Her jade eyes blinked, and she cocked her head and miaowed.

'That bad, eh?'

He opened the door and went through the hall and into the drawing room. Lights twinkled on the verandah. 'I'm sorry, my love,' he said when he found Jane out there. 'Things at the plantation took longer than I expected.'

'Never mind, Emerald invited me to tea, so I expect you're far hungrier than I am. When Constable Nadar telephoned, I told cook to start the final preparations for dinner. It should be ready soon.'

In the bathroom, de Silva stripped off his jacket and shirt and confronted the bleary-eyed face in the mirror. Perhaps he shouldn't have curtailed his earlier sleep quite so readily. He wetted and soaped a flannel and scrubbed it over his face and neck, removing the dust of the drive to the plantation. Bella, who had been prowling along the bathroom shelf stepping daintily between bottles and brushes, jumped down and removed herself to a corner, watching the operation suspiciously. He grinned. 'Don't worry. No one is going to try to wash you.'

Dried off, he put on a white cotton tunic and changed his uniform trousers for a sarong, then freed from his leather shoes, he wiggled his toes and slipped on a pair of rope sandals.

'I've poured you a whisky,' Jane called from the verandah as he came back into the drawing room. He went outside, plumped down into his chair, and took his first sip. 'Ah, that's good, thank you.'

'Well, tell me what happened this afternoon.'

He swallowed another mouthful of whisky. 'Many things. I have plenty for you to get your nose into.'

'Teeth, dear. Noses go in books.'

'Noses in books, eyes on stalks, burning ears – your language has too many odd ways of putting things for a tired Ceylonese policeman.'

'Poor dear; no more English lessons then. Back to what happened this afternoon.'

'What do you think?' he asked when he had recounted Peter Flint's story.

Jane frowned. 'Whether he's innocent or not, he's taking an enormous risk. If a jury only has his word for what happened, they'd have to be thoroughly convinced that he's an honest man. Do you know if there's anyone who could be called to attest to his good character?'

'Possibly an old employer or someone he's worked with, but in Nuala I doubt he's known to many people outside the plantation and then probably only if he's done business with them. Isobel and Marina Moncrieff would be the obvious ones to speak up for him, but if it came out that he and Marina were close, and no doubt it would, her testimony would be worth nothing.'

'Would Isobel speak up for him, do you think? Her opinion might carry some weight, despite her financial involvement.'

'A day or two ago, I would have been doubtful, but she seemed very sympathetic towards him today. She even talked of paying for him to have the best lawyers. There would certainly be people who could confirm that Donald Moncrieff had a terrible temper and a habit of insulting people.'

'I wonder if they'd come forward. People are often reluctant to speak ill of the dead.'

'You know, something that struck me about Peter Flint's

confession was the detail with which he described it. Eight years is a long time, yet he hardly hesitated.'

Jane looked thoughtful for a moment. 'I see what you mean, but on the other hand, wouldn't something so dramatic be harder to forget than an everyday occurrence?'

'I suppose it would. Fortunately, I've never had the need to test out that theory.'

Dinner was served. In the dining room, de Silva sniffed appreciatively the aromas of roasted spices, garlic, and lemongrass. The fiery orange of a fenugreek seed curry and the deep red of a beetroot one gave the table a cheerful air. Both had a subtle sweetness to which he was particularly partial. He heaped his plate and concentrated on eating for a while.

'What intrigues me about Peter Flint's confession,' observed Jane, 'is that he made it at all. He must realise what a risk he's taking. He could simply deny all knowledge of what happened to Donald.'

De Silva took a sip of his glass of water. 'Yes, but then the most likely suspect left is Marina. He may be trying to protect her.'

'Does she know he's confessed?'

'I doubt it. I haven't reported to Archie yet and I'm sure Prasanna and Nadar would have told me if he'd telephoned the station to find out what's been going on.' He helped himself to another spoonful of the fenugreek seed curry. 'Silence gives me the advantage of a free hand, but if I'm to question Marina tomorrow, I ought to give Archie the latest information.' He raised an eyebrow. 'And I suppose it will be as good a time as any to tell the dragon who guards the gate.'

Jane laughed. 'Poor Florence. She means well, you know.'

'I'm sure she does.'

After dinner they returned to the verandah and sat in companionable silence for a while before bed. The delicious fragrance of jasmine perfumed the air; comfortably replete, de Silva turned the case over in his mind.

'After I'm done at the Residence,' he said at last, 'I think it will be time to find this lady who was working as a companion to Isobel at the time Donald disappeared. I've only heard her story second hand. I want to find out if she backs up Isobel's version of it.'

'What if she doesn't? Do you think we should include Isobel in the list of suspects?'

'I'm not sure yet. We know she disliked her stepson and was aware that he ill-treated Marina, but I don't think that alone constitutes a convincing motive.'

'Mm, I suppose not. What about this telephone call Rosamund Collins claimed she overheard? Do you think it was rather flimsy evidence for Donald's disappearance?'

'It's certainly regrettable that Archie didn't go into it more at the time.'

'But why would the companion make it up?'

'That's what I hope to find out. And then there's Muttu, the head servant at the main house. When I went up there, his deputy told me that he'd gone back to his village. The deputy had no idea when he was coming back or where the village is.'

'That does sound suspicious.'

He nodded. 'I'll try to get down to Colombo tomorrow afternoon. I'm not sure if there'll be time to visit the convent then or whether it would be best to go the following morning. Either way, it's a long drive there and back in a day, so I think I'll stay the night. If there's time,' he added, 'it would be interesting to have another word with Perera. I'd like to see how he reacts if I ask him whether he thought he would escape detection when he went to the house on Saturday night.'

'If either of our theories about him being involved with the Moncrieffs are right, do you really think he'd confess it?'

'Probably not, but his reaction might be revealing.'

CHAPTER 15

He woke remembering that he still needed to speak to David Hebden about examining the bones to try to establish the cause of Donald Moncrieff's death.

'I'd like to arrange for him to do that before I go to Colombo,' he said to Jane as they ate breakfast. He looked at the clock on the dining room mantelpiece. It was almost half past eight. 'Do you think it's too soon to telephone?'

'I don't think so. Emerald says they wake early these days. I've told her it will be good practice for when the baby arrives.'

He finished his cup of tea. 'Then I'll do it now.'

When he came to the telephone, David Hebden cut short de Silva's apology. 'Interesting,' he said when de Silva finished telling him about Peter Flint's confession. 'So, I suppose you want to know if his story about how Moncrieff died is plausible.'

'That's exactly it. What do you think?'

'Did Flint tell you whereabouts on the head the impact occurred?'

'At the back.'

'And the cabinet was metal, you say.'

'Yes.'

'Hmm. A very severe, precisely targeted blow to the back of the head is capable of causing death almost instantaneously if the brain stem ruptures, and the likelihood of that increases when the surface the head impacts on is hard like metal. Did Flint say he believed that Moncrieff died immediately?'

'No. He indicated that there might have been a chance of saving him, but he panicked and didn't go for help.'

'Even if he had, if the injury was sufficiently severe, the outcome might have been the same. Imagine the human brain as a lump of jelly on a plate. If the jelly is shaken with enough force, it wobbles and eventually tears. Likewise, the brain will rebound within the skull and may tear or twist resulting in injuries. Swelling can restrict the flow of blood and the oxygen it carries to the brain. Without far more sophisticated treatment than we have available, the brain wouldn't remain alive for long.'

'If the blow caused Moncrieff's death, would you expect to find that his skull had been fractured?'

'I'd be surprised if that wasn't the case. Did Rudd notice anything there?'

'No, he mentioned the broken tibia but after that he seemed in a hurry to leave.'

'Well, if you want, I'll take a look at the bones and see if I can shed any light on matters for you.'

'I'd be most grateful if you would. The remains are at the undertakers. I'm driving down to Colombo later today, but I'll be back tomorrow evening.'

'Very well, I'll do my best to deal with it before then. At present, I don't have a long list of calls for this afternoon.'

De Silva thanked him and rang off.

'He's offered to have a look at the bones,' he said when he went back into the dining room.

'Good.' Jane lifted the teapot. 'Another cup now you've arranged that?'

'Please.'

'What did he think about Flint's account of the accident?'

'He thought that if the blow had been severe enough

to lead to death, it would very likely have caused a skull fracture.' He spooned sugar into his cup and stirred. 'I'll think I'll make a quick call to the Residence. It's time I spoke to Marina.'

It was a task he wasn't going to relish. Jane looked at him sympathetically. 'Don't worry, dear. I know questioning her will be a delicate matter, but I'm sure you'll handle it perfectly.'

'Thank you for the vote of confidence, my love. I hope it won't be misplaced.'

'Will you suggest she has someone else with her?'

'Yes.'

'She may feel happier if it's another woman,' Jane went on. 'What about Florence? I know we like to joke about her, but she's no fool, and she would be independent.'

'I'll let Marina decide.'

*   *   *

He made the call and ten minutes later set off for the Residence. Archie was in his study.

'Join me in a walk round the garden, de Silva? I usually take this chap out for a run about now.' He put a hand on Darcy's head and the Labrador gazed up at him adoringly.

De Silva was glad of the suggestion. If Archie was concerned about Marina's state of mind and the effect questioning might have on her, this might be an awkward conversation, and those were usually easier to conduct when out in the fresh air.

With Darcy lolloping ahead, they walked in the direction of the lake where Archie liked to fish. He glanced up at the cloudless blue sky. 'Too bright for fishing today,' he remarked. He adjusted the brim of his Panama hat. 'Right, you'd better fill me in on what's been going on.'

His frown deepened as de Silva explained, beginning with what he, Prasanna and Nadar had found in Peter Flint's office. He finished with his conversation with David Hebden that morning.

'Marina will have to be told about this confession, of course,' said Archie. 'I imagine you'll want to hear her side of the story and try to establish the truth. I'm sure I hardly need tell you that it would be inappropriate for you to interview her alone.'

'Of course.'

'If she wants a solicitor present, that can't be arranged at the drop of a hat.' He thought for a moment. 'But she might rather just have another woman present.'

'If so, would Mrs Clutterbuck consider it?'

'We'll turn back now. I'll go and have a word with her. I suggest you wait in the library while I sort this out.'

* * *

The library was gloomy with thick damask curtains that kept out most of the sunshine. De Silva picked up an old copy of *The Field* from a table and flipped through articles about salmon fishing and grouse shooting. The photographs showed men in tweeds and gaiters with guns crooked over their arms. Labradors and spaniels nosed their way through bracken or stood proudly with game birds dangling from their jowls. Although he disliked the idea of hunting, at least these sportsmen probably ate what they caught. The situation was different with the big game hunters who shot wild animals in Ceylon and many other places, killing purely for the sake of taking trophies. How many magnificent creatures had been needlessly sacrificed to satisfy their vanity? He remembered the tiger-skin rug that had snarled up at him from the floor of Isobel Moncrieff's drawing room and felt a shudder of revulsion.

The door opened and Florence came in. He put the magazine down and got to his feet. 'Good morning, ma'am.'

'And good morning to you. I understand from my husband that you suggested I accompany you when you meet Marina. I've spoken with her and she's in agreement. I'd like to make it clear at the outset, however, that although I've prepared her in order to avoid your news coming as a complete shock, should she become too distressed the interview will have to terminate.' She gave him a stern look.

Part of de Silva wished that she hadn't taken it upon herself to intervene. It deprived him of the opportunity to observe Marina's initial reaction, but it was done now.

'I thought my private sitting room would be a more suitable place for our meeting than the drawing room. I've asked one of the staff to bring her along. Shall we go?'

He followed her down a corridor that he'd not seen before. Instead of hunting prints and gloomy landscapes, the walls were hung with attractive watercolours of picturesque cottages and gardens.

'My late mother was an artist,' remarked Florence. 'I'm afraid my brothers and I didn't inherit her talent.' She stopped at a door. 'Here we are.'

Marina sat on the edge of a chintz-covered armchair with her hands tightly clasped in her lap. In the photograph de Silva had seen of her, her dark wavy hair framed her face and she was smiling, but today her hair was scraped back and her expression was strained. She looked up at him warily.

'Good morning, ma'am. I'm sorry that our last meeting was under such unpleasant circumstances,' he said gently.

Florence pointed to a chair. 'Why don't you sit there, Inspector?' She sat down herself with her back to a bay window that overlooked a lawn and some rose beds.

'Florence has told me that you're holding Peter at the police station,' said Marina. 'She says he's confessed to a fight with my husband that led to his death.' Her eyes filled with tears and she wiped them away with her handkerchief. 'I blame myself. I ought to have left Donald long before that. Our marriage had become a sham, but I was afraid of him. I knew Donald would be too proud to accept that I wanted to be with Peter.'

She crushed the handkerchief into a damp ball. 'But if only I'd known he'd found out about us and planned to confront Peter, I would have found the courage somehow. Donald's temper was so violent. I knew what he was capable of from my own experience.'

'Are you saying that your husband didn't tell you?'

'Yes.'

Her answer surprised de Silva. In his experience, men who suspected their wives of infidelity usually chose the easiest target first, and wouldn't that be the wife who was vulnerable and already afraid of them, rather than her lover?

'Does that surprise you?'

'I'd reached the stage where nothing about Donald surprised me.'

'Even his disappearance with no warning?'

'Donald was often absent, and he never explained where he'd been. Usually, I presumed he was with other women.' She made a face. 'There would be a hint of perfume that I knew wasn't mine, or a stray hair on his jacket. There was one rule for Donald and another for me.'

'You were told he'd left Nuala with another woman. When was that?'

Marina looked at Florence. 'When your husband came to ask if we knew where Donald was. That was when Isobel's companion admitted she'd heard him talking with this woman and making plans to go away with her.'

'The companion being Rosamund Collins?'

'I think that was her name.'

'Why was she so convinced they were planning to leave

Nuala? Did she tell you the exact words your husband used?'

'Eight years have passed, Inspector. At the time, her story was plausible.'

'But even when years passed without the faintest rumour of where he was, are you sure you never suspected your husband might be dead?'

Marina's eyes blazed. 'No. My anxiety diminished but I was always afraid that one day he would walk in the door and the misery would start all over again.' Her eyes flashed. 'I was *always* afraid he'd come back. I wish Peter hadn't kept the truth from me.'

'You must have known people would be looking for you after that. Why did you hide?'

'Peter was afraid I'd be blamed. He said he wanted time to decide what we should do.'

'Why do you think he kept the truth from you for so long?'

The colour drained from Marina's face. 'I can't explain it, but I refuse to believe he meant to kill Donald. He had to defend himself. It was an accident.'

'Nevertheless, ma'am, it is against the law to conceal a death,' de Silva said quietly.

Rising from her chair, Marina went to the window and turned her back to the room. She gripped the sill. 'I don't care about that,' she said angrily. 'All I care about is that you let him go.'

Her shoulders shook, and before de Silva had time to reply, Florence raised a hand. 'I think that's enough for now. Marina needs to rest.'

* * *

'It could have gone better,' he said gloomily as he sat on a chair in their bedroom where Jane was packing his overnight bag for him. 'I didn't even have the chance to bring up the subject of the hidden profits. I don't blame Florence. She was very restrained until Marina became upset, and she warned me she'd bring the interview to an end if that was the case.'

Jane rolled up a pair of socks and tucked them in a corner of the holdall. 'How did she seem at first?'

'Surprisingly calm and controlled. That may have been because Florence had already given her the gist of Flint's confession. If she's hiding something, that would have given her time to prepare.'

'Several things about her story strike me as odd,' said Jane, starting to fold a shirt. 'I find it hard to believe that Donald wouldn't have tried to make her give Flint up before he did anything else. As Flint was working for him, he could have sacked him at any time.'

De Silva stroked Bella, who had come into the room and started to rub up against his calf. 'But I suppose that then she might have tried to leave with Flint; maybe Donald thought she would. But I agree, that is strange.'

'And if Flint and Marina were so close, can one really believe that he kept the truth from her for eight years? Especially if she was so anxious about Donald coming back.'

She turned to put the folded shirt in the holdall and then stopped. 'Oh, Bella, what *are* you doing?'

De Silva laughed and scooped the little cat out of the holdall where she was preparing to curl up on the clothes that were already packed. He held her at arms' length, and she gave a plaintive miaow.

'Do you want to come with me? I'm afraid I don't think that would be wise. Colombo is far too busy and full of traffic for a country cat. What if I lost you?'

'I doubt she'd let you,' said Jane. 'Your little shadow.' She straightened the clothes Bella had rumpled and put in the shirt. 'Were you convinced by Marina's outburst before Florence called a halt to the interview?'

'I'm not sure. I don't feel I have her measure yet. Flint seems genuinely to care for her, but she may have been using him all these years.'

'Do you mean she killed Donald after all, and Flint is covering up for her?'

'It's something that has to be considered. If he's found guilty, it will be interesting to see what she does. Isobel thought she would inherit the plantation and everything that goes with it. She would be an independent woman then.'

'What about Isobel? She doesn't seem to have as strong a motive as Marina for wanting to be rid of Donald, but she might know more than she's admitting. The three of them may have made a pact to stay silent. All the while living very comfortably off the profits from the plantation.'

'Hmm, yes. It would be interesting to know more about Isobel's past and whether her financial affairs are as robust as she claims. If not, she would have a powerful motive for keeping quiet and taking the money.'

Jane snapped the clasp on the holdall shut. 'There, that should be enough for one night. You will telephone me when you arrive, won't you?'

'Of course.' He kissed her cheek. 'I'll miss you.'

After lunch, he telephoned Hebden's surgery, but he had been called out on an emergency after all and not returned.

'Did he happen to leave a message for me?' de Silva asked the receptionist.

'I'm afraid not. Shall I ask him to call you when he comes back?'

'There's no need. I'm sure he'll be in touch when he's ready.'

* * *

He was on the edge of town when a way of finding out more about Isobel Moncrieff's past came to him. Hadn't she said her first husband had occupied a senior position in the Justice Secretariat? Charlie Frobisher and his young lady were staying with her uncle who had also worked there. He might know of him. De Silva searched his memory for the name and after a few moments, came up with it: Harold Dacre.

A short detour took him to the main post office where he used the public telephone to call the Residence. He spoke to one of the secretaries and gave his name, then asked if they had a telephone number for Charlie in Colombo. He recalled Charlie mentioning that he always had to ensure he could be contacted by his base if they needed him to return early from leave.

He waited, listening to the muffled clack of typewriters, while the secretary looked it up.

'We only have an address, I'm afraid,' she said when she came back on the line. De Silva wrote it down and thanked her then went to the telegraph office. When he had composed his message, he gave the small hotel in Colombo where he usually stayed as the return address, paid the fee, and started out again for Colombo.

CHAPTER 16

The sun was setting over the ocean by the time he arrived, turning water and sky to startling shades of pink and purple. A cool, salty breeze blew. He decided that once he had taken a room at the hotel and deposited his bag, he would go down to Galle Face Green for a walk by the water and something to eat.

There was a message at the hotel reception from Charlie Frobisher; he took it up to his room to read it. Charlie suggested de Silva meet him outside the Galle Face Hotel at ten o'clock the next morning and promised to speak with Ruth's uncle beforehand.

It took only a few moments to unpack his bag and he was soon on his way to the green. He had been looking forward to an evening there ever since he left Nuala. Not only was the view beautiful, he knew there were also numerous stalls selling tasty food. His mouth watered at the prospect of one of the specialities that he particularly enjoyed – isso wade, prawn-topped lentil patties served with chopped chillies and onions. Just the smell of them made you think of the sea.

He bought a paper bagful and found a place to sit where he could listen to the ebb and flow of the waves whilst he ate. All along the grassy promenade, graceful coconut palms swayed in the wind like the spinnakers of sailing boats. People taking their evening strolls passed him without a glance. There were noisy groups of families and friends, young lovers too wrapped up in each other to pay much attention to the view, and older couples talking quietly or walking in companionable silence as he and Jane would have been doing. All of a sudden, he felt lonely. Colombo had been his childhood home and the place where he had spent his early career, but it was very different to Nuala. There, it was never long before you saw someone you knew. He belonged there now. In Colombo, one might go for days without seeing a familiar face.

He polished off the last of his snack then crumpling up the soiled paper bag, found a place to throw it away and walked a little further along the promenade. At one stall, a man prepared slices of mango and sprinkled them with pepper and salt, another dish that de Silva found hard to resist. He bought some and ate as he walked along, wondering what news Charlie Frobisher would have for him in the morning.

Eventually, he started to think of the hotel and the comfortable bed that awaited him. Strolling back along the green, he passed the grand façade of the Galle Face Hotel, its lights twinkling like a million candles. He and Jane had stayed there once, but tonight the Lotus Flower Hotel would be perfectly adequate.

* * *

Morning found him back at Galle Face Green a little before ten o'clock. It was even busier than it had been the previous evening with rickshaws darting in all directions and covered wagons and pack animals transporting goods. The city's port and its largest market, the famous Pettah, was a little to the east of the northern end of the Green.

People crossed the grass, intent on their own business

or pausing to chat if they met a friend. Children flew kites decorated with coloured streamers that fluttered brightly against the blue of the cloudless sky. In several areas, boys had set up stumps and were playing cricket. He watched one of the taller ones whack the ball and run like the wind between the stumps. Maybe he was a Sergeant Prasanna in the making.

'Good morning!' a voice called out. De Silva looked up to see Charlie Frobisher hurrying towards him. 'I hope I haven't kept you waiting.'

'Not at all. I've been enjoying the view.'

'Pretty different to Nuala, eh?'

'Yes,' said de Silva with a smile. 'It's pleasant to come back for a while, but I know which I prefer. I hope your stay with Ruth's uncle and aunt is going well.'

'I think I can safely say that it is. Her uncle and I hit it off pretty quickly and her aunt's a charming lady.' He grinned. 'They seem to like me as much as I like them, which is a relief. Between ourselves, I'm hoping Ruth might agree to marry me, and it would help if they approved. Her parents are both dead, and her uncle and aunt are the closest thing she has to family.'

'Then prospects look good.'

Charlie laughed. 'Of course, it's Ruth who has to decide.'

From what de Silva had seen, that wasn't likely to be a problem. He was sure Jane would be pleased to hear of Charlie's intentions.

All at once however, Charlie's expression clouded. 'The only problem is that our lives are not our own at the moment. I've got my wings now. If I'm not needed in this part of the world, there's a chance of being sent back to England to help with the war effort in Europe. I hope Ruth would wait for me, but—'

A shiver crept up de Silva's spine. The war seemed very far away. If he was honest, he had to admit that he didn't often think about it, but inevitably, it would be more to the forefront of the Britishers' minds. 'I hope your fears are unfounded,' he said gravely.

'So do I, but we shall see. Now, to business. I managed to get some time alone with Ruth's uncle and asked him about Harold Dacre. He remembered him, but he remembered Dacre's wife, Isobel, far more vividly. He said she made quite an impression when they were stationed here.'

De Silva wasn't surprised.

'But Ruth's uncle says Dacre was only a middle-ranking official, and he doubted he earned a lot. Isobel was always stylishly dressed and behaved as if they had money, but they lived in a very modest house that wasn't in a smart area of town. So, what's your interest in the Dacres?'

De Silva hesitated, then decided that as Charlie had helped him, he was owed an explanation even if he wasn't directly involved in the case.

'After she was widowed, Isobel married Victor Moncrieff, a wealthy man and father of Donald. We know for sure now that they're Donald's remains we've found.'

'How does the information about Harold Dacre help your investigation?'

'Perhaps only indirectly, but it's useful to know what Isobel's financial situation was before she married Victor. She claims that when he died, he left her well off. We know that her stepson Donald spent money very freely. When he disappeared, the story was that he'd left Nuala with a lover. Isobel claims she wanted to hide some of the profits of the plantation so that he couldn't get his hands on them and fritter them away if he returned. In the meantime, some of the profits could also be put towards improvements.'

'But why hide profits if they were being used for improvements?'

'According to the plantation manager, Peter Flint, Donald usually blocked improvements. It may be true that

Isobel and Flint though it best to do them on the quiet. In any case, Flint helped her and falsified the accounts. He turns out to have been romantically involved with Donald's widow, Marina. It's not clear whether Marina knew about the money, but certainly Flint held on to some of the hidden profits. He described it as a running away fund for him and Marina, and Isobel agreed to it. She took the rest. Who knows whether her motives were as disinterested as she claims? Now that we know Donald was never coming back because he was dead, it raises the question of whether all or any of Isobel, Flint, and Marina were responsible for his murder. Flint claims he and Donald had a fight, and his death was an accident, but I'm not sure I believe that. He may have killed Donald deliberately, possibly with the connivance of one or both of Marina and Isobel, or be covering for one of them if they're the murderer.'

Charlie frowned. 'And whether or not Marina was aware of it, all of them benefitted financially from the fiction that Donald was missing rather than dead. But after someone has been missing for as long as Donald was, I believe it's legally possible to declare they must be dead. Surely if Marina or Isobel were innocent and stood to inherit, wouldn't it suit them better to go down that route?'

'Archie mentioned that, but they obviously didn't try it. Whether it indicates guilt or lack of knowledge is hard to say. Donald's will – assuming he left one – may help us. I'll have to think of a way of locating it sooner rather than later. Isobel was sure he wouldn't leave anything to her as they got on so badly, and she reckoned everything would go to Marina, but she may be wrong. For example, Donald might change his will if he knew his wife didn't love him and was having an affair with his employee. In the meantime, it shouldn't be hard to get hold of a copy of his father's one. As he's been dead for many years, it ought to be filed at the Probate Registry here. There may be something in that too. Now Ruth's uncle has helped us to establish that it's very unlikely Isobel brought money into her marriage with Victor, I'd like to know how well off he really left her.'

'Are you going over to the Registry now?'

'I suppose I should. It may take a while to obtain a copy, but once I've ordered it, I can spend the time visiting the lady who used to be Isobel Moncrieff's companion. She was the one who told Archie she'd heard Donald making plans to leave Nuala with his lover. With luck it won't be too late by the time I'm ready to drive home. I might even pay a visit to Johnny Perera.'

'Don't tell me he's involved!'

'Most likely not, but I haven't formally ruled him out given the circumstances in which Donald's remains were found.'

Charlie looked at his watch. 'I'll tell you what, I'll order the copy of the will for you and you can get on with your interviews straight away. Ruth's aunt has taken her shopping and her uncle's busy, so I've the morning to myself. A friend of mine works at the Registry. I might even be able to hurry things along for you.'

'I'd be most grateful.'

* * *

The convent was in a peaceful square to the south of the city centre. The noonday sun glinted on its terracotta roofs and high, whitewashed walls. A few clumps of weeds and grass grew in the gutters and below them, the whitewash was stained with brownish-grey streaks; the gutters must overflow in the monsoon rains, he thought. Iron bosses studded a solid-looking wooden door with a small grille in its centre. De Silva went up and knocked.

A few moments passed then, with a scraping sound, the

shutter behind the grille slid open to reveal a nun with eyes as sharp as chips of flint.

'Can I help you?' she asked.

'I'm looking for a lady called Rosamund Collins. I believe she resides here.'

'She is one of our lay sisters. May I ask why you wish to see her?'

'I'm Inspector de Silva, head of police in the town of Nuala in the Hill Country. Miss Collins used to work there for a lady called Isobel Moncrieff. It's recently come to light that Mrs Moncrieff's stepson, Donald, died just before Miss Collins left her employment. I hasten to say there's no suggestion Miss Collins was involved, but his death has given rise to questions. I hope Miss Collins will be able to help me with answers to some of them.'

'Wait here, please.' The nun closed the grille.

De Silva sighed and settled down to wait. This being left on doorsteps was getting to be a habit. He wiped beads of sweat from his forehead and the bridge of his nose. He hoped that if he managed to get in, he would find it cooler on the other side of the nunnery walls. He wondered if the rest of the place was as plain as the exterior. How different it was from the religious buildings indigenous to Ceylon: no gold or brilliant colours, no carvings, no images. In his own Buddhist faith, monks wore saffron robes, the colour of the rising sun, not sombre black.

The minutes ticked by, and he wondered if he had been forgotten. A rickshaw trundled into the square and he hoped it would halt at the convent for its passenger to gain admittance. Perhaps he would be able to slip in along with them, but the rickshaw didn't stop. He shifted his weight from one foot to the other. Maybe it would be best to leave a message and go to the Registry to see if the copy of Victor Moncrieff's will was ready. He was still debating whether to do so when heard the rattle of bolts and the convent door opened.

The nun was short and plump and far less intimidating than her eyes had suggested she would be. 'Follow me, please,' she said. 'The Mother Superior wishes to see you first.'

A paved courtyard with a well at its centre met de Silva's eyes; the buildings that enclosed it on three sides looked as plain as the convent had from the square. The nun tucked her hands into her habit and walked in the direction of the porch opposite them, gliding so smoothly that she looked as if she were on wheels. They went inside and she led him down a narrow, high-ceilinged corridor. The air felt pleasantly cool to de Silva after his hot wait in the sun, although the austere atmosphere had a subduing effect. The place had a different smell from a Ceylonese religious building too: strong bleach with an undertone of boiled vegetables, rather than the aromas of spice and incense.

The nun knocked at one of the doors then stood aside to let him enter the room. From behind the large desk, the Mother Superior examined him. She was elderly with an angular, deeply lined face and shrewd, but not unfriendly, eyes.

'Good afternoon, Inspector de Silva. Sister Claude tells me you wish to see Sister Rosamund. Before I agree, I would like to know more about the business you have with her.'

Carefully, de Silva gave her a more detailed version of Rosamund Collins's involvement in the events surrounding Donald Moncrieff's death. He took extra pains to stress that although she might have valuable information, there was no question of her being held responsible.

The Mother Superior heard him out then nodded. 'Very well, I'll have her brought here. I think it will be more appropriate for me to be present while you have your conversation.'

Her tone brooked no argument, so he thanked her.

A few minutes later, there was a tap at the door and

Rosamund Collins arrived. She was a small woman with a face almost as pale as her coif; it was set in an anxious expression. 'You sent for me, Mother Superior,' she said timidly.

The Mother Superior's expression softened a little. 'You have a visitor, Sister Rosamund, but there's no need to be alarmed. Just answer his questions as fully as you are able.' She turned to de Silva. 'Carry on, Inspector.'

'Thank you.' He tried to smile reassuringly at Sister Collins whose pale cheeks were now flushed. 'I understand that you were working for Mrs Isobel Moncrieff in Nuala in 1932.'

'Yes, I was.' Her words were almost inaudible.

'In January of that year, her stepson left town and, since then, has not returned. When you were questioned by Assistant Government Agent Mr Clutterbuck about his departure, you claimed to have heard him speaking to a woman who wasn't his wife; you said you believed they were making plans to leave Nuala together.'

'I did. At least I thought that was what they were doing.' There was a tremor in Rosamund Collins's voice, and she glanced desperately at the closed door.

'You thought?' De Silva frowned. 'I appreciate that several years have passed, but I've been led to understand that your testimony was unequivocal at the time. Why was that?'

'I'm not sure,' stuttered Sister Rosamund. The flush deepened and her eyes looked moist.

'Can you recall anything specific that you overheard?'

'I can't—'

'Please, take your time,' he said quietly. There was a long pause. The Mother Superior sat with her hands folded on the desktop, the personification of patience. De Silva wondered what was going through her mind.

'Not his words exactly,' Sister Rosamund said at last. 'It just sounded as if that was what they were talking about.'

'How many times did you hear them talking together?'

She hesitated again. 'Twice… or perhaps it was more than twice,' she added lamely.

The Mother Superior gave her a severe look. 'Sister, I hope I don't need to remind you of your vows. You know that you must answer truthfully.'

Now the colour drained from Sister Rosamund's face. 'I'm sorry, Reverend Mother.'

'Please tell the inspector what really happened.'

Sister Rosamund's hands twisted in the folds of her habit. She reminded de Silva of a frightened deer that has just seen a leopard crouching ready to spring. 'I never heard anything,' she blurted out.

'Then why did you claim that you had?' asked de Silva.

'When Mr Clutterbuck asked me if I knew about Mr Moncrieff's disappearance, I didn't know what to do.'

'You could simply have told the truth. What stopped you?'

'I… I did know something. It would have been wrong to pretend I didn't, but—'

'But?'

'I was afraid Mrs Moncrieff, my employer, would be even angrier with me,' Sister Rosamund said meekly.

De Silva was puzzled. He knew that Isobel had been angry at having the family's secrets aired, but what circumstances could there have been to increase that anger?

'I never overheard Mr Moncrieff talking about leaving Nuala, but I did see a letter that my employer was writing to him. I didn't want to lie to Mr Clutterbuck, but I knew Mrs Moncrieff would be furious if she found out I'd read her private correspondence.'

'What was the letter about?'

'She told him that he had disgraced the family by leaving with this woman. She never wanted to see him again and he was not to contact Marina either.'

'Did you see where the letter was addressed to?'

'I can't remember.'

'Think hard, Sister,' intervened the Mother Superior.

A look of misery came over Sister Rosamund's face. She seemed to be on the verge of tears. 'I'm sorry. I only looked quickly. I was afraid I'd be seen.'

'So, you invented these telephone calls.'

She bowed her head. 'Yes, Mother Superior,' she said in a small voice.

*   *   *

As he left the convent, de Silva felt some pity for Rosamund Collins. She had helped a murderer to go free, but he was sure that had never been her intention. The conflict between the dictates of her conscience and her fear of her employer was to blame. Briefly, he considered whether Isobel had really believed Donald had eloped, and her sentiments were genuine, or whether the letter had been a ruse. Presumably in that case she had intended Collins, or someone else who would pass the information on to Archie, to see it. To de Silva, that was the most plausible scenario. He decided it was not a priority to call on Perera. Indeed, he asked himself why Perera kept popping back into his thoughts. Could it simply be that Perera didn't even consider, still less worry about, the consequences of being discovered looking for the Bugatti? Was he simply an arrogant young playboy who believed he could charm his way out of any situation? De Silva had to ask himself if he was not just a little bit jealous of the dashing young driver.

He glanced at his watch. So, yes, just the copy of the will to get now. He hoped Charlie had managed to hurry things along for him. If he had, there might be some chance of getting part of the drive back to Nuala done in daylight. All the same, he doubted he would be home in time for dinner, so he ought to telephone Jane.

First he went to the hotel to collect his overnight bag, then on to the main post office. He found a free booth and dialled the operator, asking for a reverse charge call to Sunnybank. As he waited for Jane to accept the charge, he looked at the advertisements stuck up around the booth. Two of them were for Camel and Lucky Strike cigarettes, the latter showing a man in a white doctor's coat extolling their mildness and lack of harmful effects. There were advertisements for Brylcreem and Lucky Tiger hair tonic too. From the distinctive barber-shop smell in the booth, recent occupants had been liberal users of both.

'Hello, dear,' Jane's voice came on the line. 'How are you getting on?'

'Very well.' He told her about the meeting with Rosamund Collins. 'All I need to do now is get this copy of Victor Moncrieff's will. Charlie Frobisher offered to help by ordering it while I was at the convent. I'll head over to the Registry now, but I'm afraid I won't be home in time for dinner. I'll have something to eat in Colombo before I leave.'

'Very sensible.'

He heard the pips. 'I'll ring off. This call will be getting expensive.'

'Alright, dear. Drive carefully, won't you.'

'I will.'

After he'd put down the receiver, he realised he hadn't told Jane about Charlie's confidence. She was sure to be pleased, but it would have to wait now until he got home.

He left the post office and drove to the Registry. There he found Charlie Frobisher waiting in the vast, echoing reception hall. He held out an envelope.

'Here you are. I hope you don't mind that I've taken the liberty of taking a look. I think you'll find Victor Moncrieff's will very interesting. Very interesting indeed.'

'In what way?'

'Read it yourself. It seems to set up some sort of legal trust under which the plantation and the properties on it wouldn't be inherited by Isobel or Marina on Donald's death, but by the next male descendant in the Moncrieff family.'

Swiftly, de Silva took in the implications of this news. It might mean that all three of his suspects had a compelling reason to keep Donald's death a secret. 'I'll need to have the terms of this will fully explained by a legal expert, but it may be the key to solving the case. Speed may be essential so I must get back to Nuala as soon as possible.'

'If you like, I'd be happy to ask my uncle. He should be able to clarify things.'

'Thank you, that would be a great help.'

'I'll talk to him this evening and ask him to call you first thing tomorrow.'

De Silva held out the envelope. 'Should I give you this for the moment?'

Frobisher shook his head. 'I hope you don't object, but as the additional cost was minimal, in anticipation, I ordered an extra copy.'

De Silva chuckled. 'You think of everything.'

CHAPTER 17

Jane finished studying the copy of the will and took off her reading spectacles.

'I don't really understand this trust business either, but I expect Ruth's uncle will be able to explain it. It does seem strange though for Victor Moncrieff to leave nothing at all to Isobel. Just a direction to Donald that he's to make sure she's properly looked after. It's even harder to understand when we've heard that Donald was irresponsible about money.'

'Perhaps he managed to hide that from his father.'

'I suppose so. But even if he had been prudent, Isobel was his stepmother. I think it was rash of Victor to expect him to have the same sense of responsibility towards her as he would have done if she'd been his natural mother.'

That would make no difference to an honourable man, thought de Silva. But then Donald Moncrieff had not been an honourable man. Perhaps he would have been parsimonious with his own mother too. 'The only explanation I can think of is that Victor was one of those people who believe money is always best looked after by men. Of course, there may be something in that,' he added with a grin and Jane scowled at him.

'Only joking, my love. I think Donald Moncrieff is proof that's a mistaken idea.'

Jane sighed. 'If Donald kept her short of funds, it's easy

to see why Isobel would want it to look as if he had eloped. That way, she would be safe to make her arrangement with Flint and Marina, putting herself in a much better position than she had been when Donald was around.'

She put her spectacles back on her nose and scanned the will once more. 'The address for this cousin of Donald's who now stands to inherit is an English one. I wonder if he knows about the provisions of the will. His inheritance may come as a surprise.'

'And a very pleasant one, I'm sure. Archie may know whether there are family solicitors who act for the Moncrieffs. It will be their job to track him down.'

'If Isobel is the murderer, how do you think she did it?'

'I don't have the answer to that yet. And although Peter Flint's story of how Donald died may not be true, that doesn't mean to say Flint wasn't the one who actually killed him.'

He yawned. It had been a long day and the drive back from Colombo had been a tiring one. 'It's too late now, but in the morning I'll try and speak to David. With luck, he'll have had a chance to look at the bones by now. With his help, we may be able to fit another piece in the jigsaw.'

'I wonder what Isobel would have done if Rosamund Collins had kept her mouth shut at the time.'

'Very probably she had another card up her sleeve just in case that happened. No doubt her uncharacteristic confiding in Mrs McTaggart was also part of the scheme. She'd probably heard about the trouble between Donald and McTaggart.'

'What about Marina?'

'I'm not ruling her out yet.' He thought for a moment. 'But I think there is a way that I can find out whether Flint's story about the fight and its aftermath is true without waiting to hear from David Hebden. I wish I'd considered it sooner. It's occurred to me that when I asked him why he buried Donald's body so far from where he died, he talked about using the area behind the garage courtyard because it was both accessible and private and would lose him the least time. But where we found the grave was very overgrown. I'd call it wild rather than accessible. Unless it's changed radically in the last eight years, no car would have got there and even a strong man like Flint would probably have struggled to drag Donald Moncrieff through it, especially as he was a dead weight. It wouldn't have been a quick operation.'

'What do you deduce from that?'

'That if he was primarily concerned with hiding Marina and cooking up a convincing story about how Donald died, Flint may not have got enough information from the servants to enable him to pinpoint the burial spot. It's not an easy place to find, and I doubt he had time to do that for himself before I arrested him. I think I'll take him back to the plantation. If he manages to lead me there without any help, I'll be more prepared to believe he's telling the truth.'

'I hope you aren't planning to take him up there on your own.'

'No, Prasanna can come with me. Flint's younger than I am and very probably a lot fitter. I expect he can run faster too. I don't want to give him the chance to escape. We won't manage with just the Morris, so I'll call Singh at Hatton and ask him to lend their police van and someone to drive it.'

'When will you go?'

'As soon as I can make the arrangements with Singh.'

CHAPTER 18

The promised telephone call from Ruth's uncle came the following morning while de Silva and Jane were at breakfast.

'Robert Bailey here,' a voice said cheerfully when de Silva went to take it. 'I understand from my niece Ruth's young man, Frobisher, that you need clarification of the terms of a will that he's shown me.'

'That would be a great help.'

'Well, I'll do my best not to bog you down in technicalities. Basically Victor Moncrieff, the testator as the maker of a will is called in law, used his will to put land that he owned into a trust called a settlement. I understand from Frobisher that it's a tea plantation.'

'Yes.'

'Settlement is a device used in English law to keep a landed estate in a family, almost invariably the male side of it, through the generations. The person who is entitled to benefit from the land at any one time, in this case Victor's son Donald, is known as the life tenant. In the will, the testator appoints trustees who legally hold the land and supervise the life tenant's actions to ensure that the land is properly managed and preserved, and the interests of subsequent beneficiaries protected. On the death of the life tenant, usually his eldest surviving son takes his place and so on.'

'What if the life tenant has no children?'

'The next surviving male descendant of the testator would become the life tenant.'

'And what kind of people would these trustees be?'

'Anyone whether related to the family or not, who the settlor of the land regards as a trusted advisor. In this case, it looks to be a solicitor and a senior official of a bank.'

De Silva reflected that they didn't appear to have been particularly active in their duties. 'You mentioned this settlement device is designed to protect land, but what about other assets?'

Bailey chuckled. 'Very good, Inspector. You have a lawyer's eye for detail. Other assets – shares or cash deposits for example – cannot be protected in a settlement. Therefore, Donald Moncrieff would have inherited some of his father's estate with no fetters. However, I took the liberty of checking at the Registry to ascertain the declared value of everything that Victor Moncrieff left on his death. The amount attributed to the plantation formed the bulk of it.'

De Silva thanked him and rang off then went back to tell Jane.

'So, Donald may have run through most of the assets he was free to use as he wished,' he said. 'Leaving only what the plantation made.'

'And if that wasn't doing well, he would have been hard up. Now we know Isobel was dependent on him, she definitely had a strong reason for wanting him out of the way but not declared dead. Who knows whether the cousin would have helped her.'

'The will says nothing about that. Presumably Victor assumed, not unreasonably, that Donald would outlive her. I'd better get on and call Hatton.'

Inspector Singh readily agreed to lend the Hatton van. 'I'll send my sergeant with it,' he said. 'You can rely on him to deliver your prisoner safely. How's the case going by the way?'

He listened while de Silva outlined progress.

'Well, good luck. I hope your plan is successful.'

'Thank you. Can you give me an idea of how long it will be before your sergeant gets here?'

'Give me a moment.'

He heard Singh shout someone's name then he came back on the line. 'He's on his way.'

* * *

Once the Hatton sergeant arrived, and having escorted Flint to the van, de Silva sent Prasanna with them to show the way to the plantation. He had not told Flint the purpose of the journey and had instructed Prasanna not to discuss it. If Flint was lying, de Silva didn't want to give him time to make up a more plausible story. He was getting into the Morris to follow them when Nadar emerged from the police station and hurried over.

'A call from Doctor Hebden, sir,' he puffed. 'I thought you'd want to take it.'

'I do. Well done, Constable.'

In the public room, he picked up the receiver.

'Sorry to hold you up, old chap,' said Hebden.

'That's quite alright.'

'Your constable was sure you'd want a word. Well, I've had a good look. As well as the fractures to the tibia, the body has several broken ribs, but I can't be sure of what caused the injuries. They may have happened when Moncrieff was alive, say a bullet or a heavy impact of some kind, but I'm afraid the length of time that's elapsed since the death makes a firm theory impossible. What I expect you'll be far more interested to hear is that I found no fractures to the skull. I can't say for sure that it definitely rules out your friend Flint's story, but if he's telling the truth about the severity of the blow, it's surprising.'

De Silva frowned. 'That certainly is interesting. Many thanks for taking a look.'

'My pleasure.'

* * *

Prasanna and the Hatton sergeant were waiting for him at the plantation's courtyard.

'Shall I let the prisoner out now, sir?' the Hatton sergeant asked.

'Yes.'

De Silva wasn't sure it had been entirely necessary to keep Flint sweltering in the back of the police van. Perhaps Inspector Singh was a stickler for nothing being done by his men without superior authorisation. He always seemed pretty easy-going when they encountered one another, but he might present a different face to his subordinates.

Flint emerged from the van, gulping down air and throwing them a baleful look. His handcuffs rattled as he thrust his clenched fists in de Silva's direction.

'Are you going to tell me what the hell's going on?' he snapped. 'I'm bundled into a van without a word of explanation then half roasted alive. I demand to be taken back to Nuala and I want to see a solicitor.'

He wasn't seriously the worse for wear, thought de Silva wryly, and he was entitled to have a solicitor, but first they had better get on with what they'd come to do.

'This won't take long, I assure you, Mr Flint. Since there's been considerable movement in the soil around the burial area, I need to know from you what the configuration was at the time when you disposed of the body.'

Flint looked bemused. 'What the hell do you—'

De Silva raised a hand to silence him.

'All will be revealed, Mr Flint. I promise you. Now, would you please lead us to the site?'

Flint glanced around the open spaces surrounding the courtyard, letting his eyes stop at an opening in the trees. It went in a different direction to the one that Rudd had used to take them to Moncrieff's grave, but it appeared to be wider and more navigable, probably a recent animal track. De Silva waited, hoping Flint would be sufficiently uncertain about what was going on to make a move.

The manager grunted. 'Very well.'

As he walked in the direction of the more navigable pathway, de Silva touched Prasanna's arm. 'You walk behind him,' he said. 'I doubt he'll try to make off up here, but in case he does, you can run faster than me.'

Prasanna grinned then straightened his expression. 'Righto, sir.'

Thankfully, the pathway was far less thorny and treacherous than the one Rudd had taken them down. They walked for five minutes until de Silva noticed that Flint's steps were faltering. The trees on either side of the path were still close together. It would have been difficult to step off it and up ahead, there was no promise of change. Raucous noises overhead made him look up. A troop of monkeys were swinging through the canopy, chattering and looking down at them. It brought Hamish McTaggart's garden and his target practice back to de Silva's mind. Mrs McTaggart's gossipy nature had been another piece of good luck for Isobel.

He peered into the distance once more. Was that light he saw? Slowly, the trees thinned out and the pathway widened. Flint was looking increasingly agitated. Then all at once, they emerged into open space. They were on the lip of a sheer drop that plummeted more than a hundred feet to the jungle below.

Flint turned to face them, his expression hovering between despair and defiance.

'I think we have just established that you did not bury Donald Moncrieff's body, Mr Flint,' said de Silva. 'Now, I suggest you tell us what really happened.'

CHAPTER 19

Flint slumped down on a fallen tree trunk and held out his handcuffed wrists. Sweat was pouring off him. 'Take these off, will you? I swear I won't try to make a run for it.'

De Silva gestured to Prasanna, who stepped forward and removed the cuffs. Flint wiped a freed hand across his face leaving streaks of dirt on his tanned skin. He ran his tongue over his lips. Arms folded, de Silva, Prasanna, and the Hatton sergeant stood and watched him.

'I invented the story of the fight,' he said at last. 'I've no idea who killed Donald or how they did it.'

'Why did you decide to take the blame?'

A spasm of pain crossed Flint's face. He jumped to his feet and de Silva tensed, ready to grab him, but he had only stood up to get away from the red ants that were already crawling over his trousers. He swatted them away.

'Marina. It was because of her.'

'But you said just now that you had no idea who killed Donald.'

'I don't. I…' He slammed his fist into the palm of his other hand and took a few paces away from them. De Silva glanced at Prasanna and was pleased to see he was ready to run if it became necessary, but Flint didn't go any further.

'When Donald's body turned up, I was pretty sure she'd had nothing to do with it, although after the way he treated her, I wouldn't blame her if she had, but there was still a trace of doubt in my mind. And one thing I was sure of was that she would be the prime suspect. I wanted to protect her, so I told her to stay hidden at my place while I figured out what to do.'

'Do you still have doubts?' asked de Silva.

'No. I'm convinced she's innocent.'

'If that's the case, I find it hard to believe that you've not speculated about the true identity of the murderer.'

Flint raised an eyebrow. 'Of course I have.'

'His stepmother, Isobel?'

'Precisely, though how she would be able to do it and get rid of the body beats me. I knew she didn't like him, and she was pretty quick to persuade Marina and me to come to an arrangement over finances after Donald disappeared. Marina was fairly certain Isobel wasn't well off. She'd heard her and Donald rowing about money. Namely, Donald keeping her short of it.'

'You do realise that by doctoring the accounts and diverting the hidden profits, you were committing theft?'

Flint grimaced. 'If you must put it that way.'

'It's the way the law will see it, Mr Flint. There's also the matter of your attempt to pervert the course of justice.'

Flint heaved a sigh. 'I know, I know. I'll have to take whatever's coming to me. All I care about is that Marina's safe.'

De Silva studied him. Some instinct told him that Flint was at last telling the truth. He nodded to the Hatton sergeant. 'Cuff him and take him to the van.'

'Shall I go too, sir?' asked Prasanna.

'No, stay here for a moment.'

As the Hatton sergeant marched Flint away, de Silva waited until they were out of earshot before he spoke. 'Right, Prasanna, I want you to accompany them to the station and lock Flint up, but once you've done that, leave Nadar in charge and come back here. I want to find Donald

Moncrieff's Bugatti. Presumably Flint also lied about destroying it, and I believe I know where it is. Once I've had a look, I'll go back to the Morris and wait for you.' He explained where he would leave the car. 'With luck, I'll have the last piece of evidence and it will be time to pay another visit to Isobel Moncrieff. I may need you.'

* * *

After the trek back to the place where they had left the Morris and the Hatton van, de Silva watched it bump away with Flint safely stowed inside, then headed for Isobel Moncrieff's bungalow. He parked the Morris out of sight in the spot where he'd left it on the evening before his trip to Colombo. Taking the bolt cutters that he'd put in the car before he left Sunnybank that morning, he started to walk. He hoped he would remember the way to the wooden building he'd seen. It was notoriously easy to lose oneself in even a small patch of jungle and the route might look different in daylight. Fortunately, however, it wasn't long before he caught a glimpse of the building through the trees.

Soon he stood in front of the padlocked doors. He studied the chain and frowned. The links were chunkier than he remembered. Still, he would have to make the best of what he had. He hoisted the bolt cutters, clamped the jaws around the chain and squeezed. Nothing happened. Gritting his teeth, he exerted more force until his muscles ached and pinpricks of light danced in front of his eyes, but still the chain held.

Take a breather then try again. He put the bolt cutters down, mopped his face with his handkerchief and rubbed his hands on his trouser legs to dry them. When he was ready, he clamped the bolt cutters around the chain once more. This time he felt it yield a little. One more burst of effort and it broke, its links rattling as they pooled on the ground. He opened the doors and a wave of trapped hot air billowed out to meet him. He smiled grimly. Now to see if he was right.

Even with both of the double doors open, the inside of the building was dimly lit. A large, sinister grey shape with an animal look to it crouched in the middle of the space. Half expecting it to open fiery eyes and roar, he approached cautiously, the thin covering of straw on the floor crackling under his feet. Tentatively, he reached out to touch the shape and his fingers met something stiff with a slightly greasy quality to it: a tarpaulin.

Dust that had probably lain undisturbed for years rose in clouds as he hauled it off what was underneath. It filled his throat and nostrils and more than once, a fit of coughing made him pause, but at last he saw shining chrome and gleaming paintwork. He stood back from the mound of canvas to admire the silver Bugatti, so lost in contemplation that it was only when it was too late that he sensed movement behind him. He swung round and saw a dark figure silhouetted against the light. It kicked away the broken chain and slammed shut the double doors. There was the scrape of bolts shooting across. Trapped in the darkness, he remembered he'd noticed that the shed had no windows. He would have to find his way back to the doors and try to force them but where were they? It was alarming how easily darkness disorientated one.

He stifled a yell as he bumped against something hard. There was a loud crash that reverberated in the closed space and suddenly a sickening smell of petroleum. His blood thrummed in his ears and his stomach roiled. He must pull himself together. The car: that was the answer. If he felt his way along it, he was bound to find the doors eventually.

The metal felt cool to the touch as he edged along. The tarpaulin hampered his every step and more than once he stumbled, but at last, he felt the rubber of a wheel. Level with his feet, there was a thin streak of light. Two more steps and he touched wood.

He lay down on the ground and put his mouth to the gap at the bottom of the door in an attempt to catch a breath of fresh air, but the smell of petrol still sickened him. It seemed an eternity before he heard voices. With a mixture of apprehension and hope, he strained to listen; they sounded familiar. He began to shout. A few moments later, he heard the bolts being drawn back and the doors opened. Gasping, he tumbled into the daylight.

* * *

He looked ruefully at the metal drum overturned on the floor. Rust and corrosion had worn it eggshell thin, and it sat in a black, treacly puddle of leaking petrol. It was a mercy no one had tried to drive the Bugatti out of the building. The merest spark from the ignition, and in no time the whole place would very likely have been ablaze. He brushed straw from his hair, trying to compose his face into a dignified expression. It wouldn't do for his juniors to see him in such a dishevelled state.

'I'm sorry we weren't here sooner, sir,' said Prasanna. 'We saw your car parked, but we had a bit of trouble finding you.'

'You did well. Thank you both.'

'Did you see who shut you in, sir?' asked Prasanna.

De Silva shook his head. 'But I've a good idea it was Isobel Moncrieff's servant, Jamis. We'd best get up to the house and hope we're not too late to catch the birds before they fly.'

CHAPTER 20

It was eerily quiet at the bungalow. De Silva wondered if Isobel had already left. If she had, she couldn't have much of a start, but before trying to follow he had better check inside. He beckoned to the two sergeants.

'Prasanna, you take the back and make sure no one escapes that way.' He turned to the Hatton sergeant. 'You stay here and watch the front while I go inside.'

He was about to ring the bell when he noticed that the door was ajar. Pushing it a little further open, he prepared to face an assailant, but there was silence. He stepped cautiously into the hall, keeping his back to the wall and treading as softly as possible. He had no desire to succumb to another surprise attack. Isobel's study was deserted and there was no sound from the drawing room. He reached the door and paused, then he heard her voice.

'Come in, Inspector. I presume it is you.'

He stepped into the room and she smiled at him. 'I wondered how long it would be before you arrived. I'm all alone, so I'm afraid I can't offer you any refreshment.'

Briefly, de Silva was nonplussed by her calmness.

'Have you come to arrest me?'

He recovered his equanimity. 'Yes; for the murder of your stepson, Donald Moncrieff. I believe you killed him and hid the body, arranging matters to look as if he'd left his wife for another woman.'

Isobel laughed. 'How clever of you to work it out. Jamis told me that you found Donald's Bugatti too. Oh, by the way, I suggest you don't waste time looking for Jamis. I let him go as soon as he told me he'd locked you in with the car. I presumed you'd soon free yourself somehow. I want you to know that I have no regrets. Victor forced me to depend on Donald's generosity – a quality foreign to his nature. Donald wanted me to beg for every penny. One day we had a more violent argument than usual, and I realised that killing him was the only option.'

She spoke with such conviction that it was easy for de Silva to believe she was untroubled by remorse.

'Who else knew about it?'

'Not Marina, I assure you. Peter Flint may have had an inkling of what happened, but he never challenged me. The only one who knew the truth was Jamis. He buried the body on my orders. As for that little mouse Rosamund Collins, and that blabbermouth Elspeth McTaggart, children would have been harder to manipulate.'

She rose from her chair and went to the window. 'I shall miss all this,' she said wistfully as she gazed out over the garden. 'Perhaps I should have made my escape when you found Donald's remains, but I couldn't let go of the hope that the furore would die down and be forgotten. My mistake was to assume that you would not be as eager to gloss over matters as Archie Clutterbuck was all those years ago.' She turned back to face him and smiled. 'If you have a fault, Inspector, it is that you are too thorough.'

De Silva wasn't sure whether she intended a compliment.

'Will you permit me a few minutes alone before I come with you? There's something I wish to do before I say goodbye to my home.'

In the normal course of events, de Silva would have insisted that anyone he had just arrested remain in his sight, but something in Isobel's tone made her hard to deny.

'Very well, ma'am. But I should warn you that I have my officers on watch outside.'

'I assure you, I'm not in the habit of running away.'

He watched her as, unhurriedly and with her head held high, she walked out of the room. It seemed to diminish without her presence. He noticed that the turquoise and rose Persian rug was not as fine as he'd thought when he first saw it. In several places, there were badly worn patches. The edge of one of the silk curtains that swept to the floor was frayed and some of the porcelain ornaments chipped. He remembered Jamis's words: *the memsahib always dresses for dinner.* There was something rather sad about the idea. Isobel Moncrieff's hold on the life she wanted must often have been precarious, and now that life would be denied her for ever.

The silence thickened, broken only by the tick of the ormolu clock on the mantelpiece. He glanced at the time. He would give her five more minutes.

Then the shot he had been half expecting rang out.

CHAPTER 21

Sunnybank
Several weeks later

After the day of Isobel Moncrieff's death, at the invitation of Florence and Archie, Marina stayed on at the Residence. Now, however, she was free to come and go as she pleased. Peter Flint remained in custody for a while until Archie, in consultation with William Petrie, the government agent down in Kandy, ruled that he would not be prosecuted, although he would have to pay back the money he took from the plantation. Archie took pains to brief de Silva fully on their discussion.

'He even expressed regret for the fact that Donald's fate hadn't been more thoroughly investigated at the time,' de Silva said to Jane.

'I should hope so. It would have saved a lot of trouble. If the matter had been left as it was, justice would never have been done.'

'Hindsight is a wonderful thing, my love.'

'And so is foresight.'

De Silva smiled. 'You know, when the charges against Peter Flint were dropped, I was conflicted. He engaged in criminal acts and has not had to face justice, according to Archie a prosecution not being deemed to be "in the public interest". On the other hand, when he was released from custody, I was rather sorry to lose his company. We talked several times and he's an interesting man. I believe he truly loves this country, and unlike many Britishers, wants to protect our wildlife, not shoot it. He's a talented artist too. He did some impressive sketches with the materials Marina brought in for him to keep him occupied.'

One of the servants came to the door of the verandah. 'Visitors are here, memsahib,' she said to Jane.

'Who are they, Leela?'

'Memsahib Moncrieff and Sahib Flint. They say they would be grateful if you have a few minutes to speak with them.'

'Of course; ask them to come in.'

The last time de Silva had seen Marina, she had been pale and troubled, but today she looked happy and relaxed in a white shirt-waisted dress that showed off her slender figure and lustrous dark hair. Peter Flint looked happy too. De Silva got to his feet.

'Forgive us for arriving uninvited,' said Marina. 'But we're leaving Nuala soon and before we go, we wanted to thank you.'

'That's very good of you, ma'am, but I was only doing my duty.'

'All the same, without you, Peter and I might have been separated for ever.'

They sat down and Jane had tea brought out. Billy and Bella woke from their afternoon doze to inspect the new arrivals, Billy his usual confident self, whereas Bella was a little shy. Flint bent down and held out his hand to her. 'My family always had cats when I was growing up. These two are quite young, I assume.'

'Yes, it seems only yesterday that they were kittens,' said Jane. 'So, where will you go when you leave here?'

'Down south to Yala. I've been offered a job at the wildlife sanctuary there. I hope to be able to make myself useful.'

'I'm sure you will.'

'I'm looking forward to it too,' said Marina. She smiled at Flint. 'The change will be good for us both.'

'So, what will happen to the plantation?' asked de Silva.

'The solicitors have been in touch with Donald's cousin who inherits it. He has no plans to leave England, so he'll put a temporary manager in to run the place until it can be sold.'

'We've heard Johnny Perera is interested,' said Flint. 'Apparently, he has a hankering to be the owner of the place where he grew up. He doesn't seem put off by its recent history, and he's already made Donald's cousin an offer for the Bugatti.'

The combination of Perera and the Bugatti would certainly add excitement to the Nuala scene, thought de Silva. He was glad he had stepped back from pursuing Perera when he did.

'As I expect you know, there's still no sign of Muttu or Jamis,' Flint added. 'But I was glad to hear that Perera intends to take on the rest of the house staff and the plantation workers.'

Half an hour later the visitors took their leave. 'It's good to see them looking so happy,' said Jane. 'They seem well suited, but they need to learn to trust as well as love each other. Particularly on Flint's side.'

'What do you mean?'

'It was noble of him to make his false confession to protect Marina, but I think he was wrong to make the decision on his own. I'm convinced that if she'd known what he was planning, she would have insisted they hold out to prove her innocence and that Isobel would have been unmasked as the murderer that much earlier.'

De Silva considered the proposition. 'You may be right,' he said thoughtfully. 'Although I suspect Flint hadn't even decided to make the confession until after he was arrested.'

'Luckily for them both, everything worked out well, but it might so easily not have done.'

* * *

Two days after the visit, he arrived home to find a parcel in the hall.

'It's addressed to you, dear,' said Jane. 'Are you expecting something?'

He shook his head. 'No, I can't imagine what it is.' He undid the string and brown paper. Inside were several more layers of wrapping. He peeled them away to reveal a framed watercolour.

Jane clapped her hands. 'Oh, how lovely! It's of Billy and Bella.'

De Silva studied it; the signature was Peter Flint's.

'I see what you mean about him being a talented artist,' said Jane. 'He's captured them perfectly, even though he saw them only briefly. He must have a very good memory. I suppose he and Marina will have left Nuala by now. We'll have to find out how to reach them in Yala and write to thank them.' She paused. 'I do hope the change of scene will be a success as they hope.'

'I expect it will be, and that reminds me, I've been thinking that it's a long time since we had a holiday. Being in Colombo reminded me of how pleasant it is to be by the sea. What do you say to a trip down south to visit Galle for a change? It's a charming town and there are beaches nearby to explore.'

'That's a marvellous idea.'

'It will mean Prasanna and Nadar having to manage on their own for a few days, but it will do them no harm to take on some extra responsibility. After all, I'm not getting any younger. One day, they will have to take charge in Nuala for good.'

Jane smiled. 'Whatever would you do with yourself, dear?'

He grinned. 'Get under your feet, I suppose. But there's no cause for alarm, I don't intend to hand in my badge just yet.'

Printed in Great Britain
by Amazon